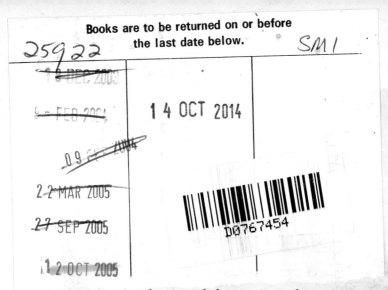

(An earlier book, *Astrid the Au Pair from Outer Space* won the Smarties Silver Medal.)

When Mum threw out the Telly is her second title for Orchard Books. She would like to say that she herself threw out the family telly – but that would be a lie. "However," she says, "the picture is very bad."

Emily lives with her husband and three children in Oxfordshire. She is currently writing a trilogy about pigs.

For Kate

Also by this author

What Howls at the Moon in Frilly Knickers?

ORCHARD BOOKS
96 Leonard Street, London EC2A 4XD
Orchard Books Australia
32/45-51 Huntley Street, Alexandria, NSW 2015
First published in Great Britain in 2003
ISBN 1 84121 810 3
A paperback original
Text © Emily Smith 2003
The right of Emily Smith to be identified as the author
of this work has been asserted by her in accordance with the
Copyright, Designs and Patents Act, 1988
A CIP catalogue record for this book is available
from the British Library.
Printed in Great Britain
1 3 5 7 9 10 8 6 4 2

when mum threw out the telly

e.f. smith

ORCHARD BOOKS

Contents

Unplugged!

Too much television is bad for you. That's what they say.

But Jeff did not agree with this.

Jeff thought there was no such thing as too much television.

Jeff watched anything. Everything. Some things more than other things.

But anything was better than nothing.

Jeff really liked television. It was so much more interesting than *life*.

Cartoons were more exciting than life.

Sit-coms were funnier than life.

And in life you never got to watch someone riding a bike over an open sewer.

Jeff studied the listings each morning to see what he was going to watch that day.

And sometimes at night he even *dreamt* television.

Mum complained, but it didn't make any difference.

He didn't take any notice of her. Which was a mistake...

One evening, late in the summer, he was watching an American cop show. The two cops were sitting in their car doing surveillance. They both had a cup of coffee (or "*corrffee*" as they called it) and were sitting there chatting.

Jeff stared at the screen.

The cops kept glancing at the building opposite. And they talked – mainly about someone called Lara, who seemed to be the fat cop's wife. Three little kids were playing on the sidewalk nearby.

Something was going to happen.

Jeff frowned. There was a distracting voice to the side of him. Mum's.

He watched as the camera zoomed in on the run-down building under surveillance. Nothing. No one. No movement at all.

Then a shot of the children talking, their heads close.

Something was going to happen. Maybe where he least expected it...

"Jeff!"

"Mmm?" He glanced up. Mum was still there.

Perhaps the cops would see something. Or perhaps something would see them...

"Weren't you listening?" she asked.

"Er..." Jeff looked back at the screen. The picture was back to the two cops in the car now.

Something was going to happen.

"I was asking you what you wanted for supper?

"Jeff! Answer!"

"Ummm."

"Answer!"

"Ummm."

"ANSWER!"

"Ummm."

And then something did happen.

Mum unplugged the television, took it up to her bedroom – and locked it in her cupboard.

Alison Pringle's Hair

Jeff pulled on his new school shoes. They felt tight after his old trainers – quite a nice feeling, really.

He was looking forward to the new term. Frankly he was bored – especially since Mum had locked up the telly.

Yup! Though he would never admit it, he was pleased to be going back to school. But he knew it wouldn't be the same without Dan.

His mate Dan – his great mate Dan – had moved to America. Dan had started school more than a week ago. And he had a Stars and Stripes flag at the corner of his classroom. He probably already said "pants" instead of "trousers".

Jeff frowned as he tightened his laces. He wasn't quite sure what he was going to do about friends. Last year, as well as having Dan, he had also been on the edges of a gang. And not just any gang. The Ryan Fuller Gang. Ryan and Al and Ben.

But he hadn't quite felt like ringing one of them up over the summer. Not even Al, who was the one he thought he liked most.

So this year, was he going to be in the Ryan Fuller Gang? Or was he going to be...out?

"It *is* sort of cool!" Ryan was saying, as Jeff caught them up at break.

"*Well* cool!" said Al.

"Particularly the cyber-battles," put in Ben.

"Yeah!" said Al.

"I suppose they fight something different every time," said Ryan.

"Must do," said Ben.

"It can't be killer druids every time," said Al. "I mean, the surprise would wear off after a bit, wouldn't it?" He put his hands up. "Aaaaargh – it's...yes, killer druids...again!"

Jeff gave a half-laugh, but Ryan was staring at Al. "*What?*"

"Well, they can't, can they? They can't have killer druids every time."

Now Ryan started laughing, and Ben joined in. "Killer druids? They weren't killer druids, you dope! They were killer DROIDS."

"Oh," said Al. "I did wonder why they weren't wearing dresses."

Killer droids? Dresses? What were they on about?

Ryan was holding an imaginary gun, eyes narrowed. Slowly and silently, he swung round the whole playground. At the end of the arc he stopped, and his eyes narrowed even further. Jeff looked to see where he was aiming. It was Henry, who was new this year in their class. He was standing over by the science block wall.

"He's not a droid!" objected Ben.

"How do you know?" said Ryan.

"He *could* be a droid," said Al.

"His hair is a bit droid-like," said Ben.

"And he's a bit of a brainiac," said Al.

"He is, is he?" said Ryan grimly. And he fired.

*

Jeff caught up with his friends again at the lunch queue.

"He wasn't too good at the hyper-drive, was he?" he heard Ben say. Or something like that.

"Reckon it was more difficult than it looked," said Al.

"Reckon it wasn't," said Ryan.

Jeff looked up towards the front of the queue. "Have you noticed Alison Pringle's hair? It's gone all frizzy."

Nobody looked at Alison Pringle's hair.

"I think I preferred it straight," Jeff said.

Still no one looked at Alison Pringle's hair. Or him, for that matter.

"Reckon it *was*," said Al.

"Reckon it wasn't," said Ben.

Ryan picked up a tray and made a face. "Shepherd's Pie! First day back and they give us Shepherd's Pie."

"There's salad as well," said Jeff.

Ryan prodded him with the corner of his tray. "Yeah, right," he said.

"Ooh, salad!" said Ben in a stupid voice. "Can't wait for me salad!"

"Hope they don't run out of cucumber!" said Al.

"Or beetroot!" said Ben.

"Or radishes!" said Al.

"Especially radishes!" said Ben.

They shuffled forwards in silence. Al put his tray on the runners, and made "DJ" moves over it with his hands.

Then Ryan said, "Wonder what they'll come up with tomorrow?"

No one said anything.

"Spaghetti?" said Jeff.

It wasn't such a bad guess, so why were they looking at him like that?

"I'm not talking about school meals!" snapped Ryan.

"Oh," said Jeff.

"I don't spend my whole time talking about school meals!"

"No," said Jeff.

"I'm talking about the next episode of *Cybernauts*!"

"Oh!" said Jeff. And he clicked.

It Gets Worse

Jeff walked into the kitchen, and threw his school-bag onto the table. A book fell out and dropped to the ground.

"Bang!" said Minna. She was sitting on the floor nearby, playing with some bricks.

"Can we get the telly out tonight, Mum?" said Jeff.

"No," said Mum.

"Tomorrow?"

"No," said Mum.

"Next Tuesday?"

"No," said Mum.

"Look, Mum," said Jeff. "There's this thing I have to watch."

Mum was now doing something at the sink. She didn't say anything.

Jeff drew a breath. "We *have* to get the telly

out and we *have* to get it out by tomorrow night...because I *have* to watch this programme."

"We can't," said Mum.

Jeff grabbed his school-bag to go for the door, changed his mind, and dumped the bag back on the table again. Another book dropped out.

"Bang!" said Minna.

"What do you mean – we can't?" said Jeff.

Mum turned around, and delivered her bombshell.

"I've lent it to someone."

He stared at her. "*Lent* it to someone?"

"Yes."

"Lent it to who?"

"An old lady."

"An old lady?" Fury rose within him. "Well, why doesn't this old lady get her own telly? Why does she have to have ours? Who *is* she, anyway?"

"You don't know her."

Jeff sat down on a chair, and sighed. "So when is she giving us back our television?"

"I said she could have it for a few months."

A few months! Mum had said it as matter-of-factly as a few *minutes!* "But, Mu-u-u-m!" cried Jeff. "There's this new *Cybernauts* thing everyone's raving about. I've *got* to watch it!"

Mum started rummaging in the freezer.

Jeff looked down at Minna, who was now stirring the bricks around a saucepan with a wooden spoon.

"Makin' tea!" she said brightly. "Bicks! *Nice!*"

He just looked at her.

She held up a yellow brick. "Wanna lalla bick, Deff? Or a geen bick?"

"I don't want a bick!" he said.

Mum came out of the freezer with a packet, and emptied it into a baking tray.

Jeff breathed out a sigh. "We have to have a telly, Mum."

Mum looked at him. "No we don't. And I'll tell you why." She said he watched too much – and Minna was beginning to watch too much too. She had been reading up about television and its effect on children. And when Mum read up, Mum *read up*. Big time.

The way she put it, the television was

17

more-or-less hoovering his brain out as he watched. "And I can *see* it, Jeff! You sit there, in some sort of…trance!"

Jeff put his head in his hands.

"And that flicker!" Mum went on.

"Ficka!" said Minna.

Jeff raised his head. "Well, that's Minna's fault, that flicker! She fiddles with the controls!"

"Not *that* flicker," said Mum. "The permanent flicker."

"What?"

"The *permanent* flicker. The picture's one big flicker."

"Ficka!" said Minna.

"Some experts say it ruins your concentration." Mum waved a spoon in the air. "Makes you—"

"*Ficka!*" said Minna.

Jeff turned on her. "Shut up, Minna!"

She gazed back at him mildly.

"*And* it's bad for your language skills!" said Mum.

Jeff stared at her. "Yer-*what?*"

Mum sighed. "So we're going to do without for a bit."

"But what about this programme? Everyone's watching it. Everyone!"

"So?" Mum spread her hands. "Be different!"

"But I don't want to be different!" wailed Jeff. "I want to watch *Cybernauts*!"

Fatsia Japonica

Jeff divided life into "Before" and "After".

"Before" was Before Mum Unplugged The Telly.

And "After" was After Mum Unplugged The Telly.

And there was no doubt about it. "After" sucked.

He missed the television, their television – his television. It was a friend. Companion. Entertainer. Hobby.

It never answered back. Or messed up your stuff. Or made you tidy your room.

Once or twice he stared sadly in the corner of the room where the telly had been. Mum had put a pot plant – a pot plant! – in its place.

There is a limit to the amount of time you

can stare at a *Fatsia Japonica*. It doesn't even have advertisements.

Sometimes he got angry with Mum, and sometimes he got angry with the old lady who had his television. He was feeling quite anti old lady nowadays. Once or twice he even glared at an old lady in the street. Maybe *she* was the one who had nicked his telly!

"Those spiders were quite lifelike…" said Al thoughtfully.

"Except about a thousand times bigger!" said Ryan.

"And hairier," said Ben.

"I'm not mad about spiders," admitted Al.

"Well, you're a wuss!" said Ryan.

"Oh, I'm not *scared* of them!" said Al. "It's just those hairy legs…scuttling along…after you…"

Ben looked thoughtful.

"If I'd been the Cybernaut, I'd have cut the web," he said.

"No! You'd have fallen off!" said Ryan.

Ben shrugged. "He was a crack fighter, though."

"I thought he was quite good," said Al.

"What did you think of it, Jeff?" Ben was looking at him.

"Um...I don't know."

"You must have seen it?" said Ryan.

"No."

"You must!"

"Gotta keep with the times, boy!" said Ben.

"It's...called...*Cyb...er...nauts*," said Ryan very, very slowly.

"Er...yeah..."

Jeff turned briskly into his gateway.

He squared his shoulders, and strode up to his front door. This time, he meant business. He opened the door, and stepped inside. "*Mum?*"

There was an answering call from upstairs. "Hi, Jeff! We're up here!"

"I'm up 'ere too, Deff!"

Jeff bounded upstairs. Mum and Minna were sitting on the bathroom floor, sorting clothes from the drier into piles.

"Mum." Jeff leant against the doorway. "We

22

need to talk."

"That would be nice." Mum shook out some jeans, and folded them.

"Deff's!" said Minna. (That was the way Minna helped Mum – saying who the clothes belonged to.)

Mum put them into Jeff's pile.

"It's about this television thing," said Jeff.

Mum pulled a big black t-shirt from the basket.

"Mumma's!" shouted Minna.

"This no television thing is getting to be a big problem," said Jeff.

"Mmm?" said Mum.

"Yes. This programme I talked about. *Cybernauts*. I really, really need to watch it."

"*Need* to?" said Mum.

"Yes."

"For school, you mean?"

There was a short silence.

"Well…" said Jeff slowly. "I reckon it's quite good for…um…physics?"

Mum laughed. "Nice try, Jeff!" She picked up some socks. "Tell you what, I'll take you to the Science Museum. Now that would be good for physics."

"Dunno dose socks," said Minna.

"OK." Jeff gave a long breath out. "The real problem is that my friends keep talking about this programme, and saying it's fantastic."

"I wouldn't worry," said Mum. "They'll stop, you'll see. They'll be on about something else tomorrow."

Jeff shook his head. "I don't think so."

Mum pulled a small pair of tights from the basket, and started putting them on Minna's head. "Not dere!" shouted Minna delightedly. "Not onna head!"

"Oh, Mum!" cried Jeff. "Aren't you bothered about my street cred at all?"

"Street cred." Mum turned to him thoughtfully. "What do you mean by that?"

"You *know*!" Mum could be *so* annoying. "How I look to others!"

"How you look to others? Hmmm." Mum leant towards him. "I'm more interested in how you look in here..." And she gently patted the side of his head.

24

Jeff tossed his head to shake her hand away.

Mum picked up a pair of Jeff's underpants.

"Deff's nickies!" shouted Minna.

Staring into Space

Life went on without television. It didn't *stop*.

But it was odd.

Weekdays were odd.

What do you do after school if you don't have a television?

OK, there's a bit of homework – but what else?

More often than not, the answer seemed to be – staring into space. (Perhaps Jeff was simply used to staring.)

Yes, weekdays were odd.

But weekends were oddest of all. *Acres* of TV-less time…

That Saturday they went to the park. Jeff took his football along. When he got there, he looked around for a tree. He had once read about a football star who learnt his ball control as a lad by kicking a ball endlessly against a tree. He found a nice thick one, and got going. But Jeff found that playing with a tree, however nice and thick, got boring after a bit.

He was just retrieving his ball, when he thought he saw Henry from his school. New Henry. Wasn't that him, walking along a path about 200 metres away? Jeff straightened up, and gazed at the figure with narrowed eyes. Yes, it *was* Henry. He seemed to be on his own. He had something in his hand. Or rather, he had something *on* his hand. Yes, it was – Jeff's eyes widened – a baseball mitt. What was Henry doing with a *baseball mitt?* Henry didn't strike Jeff as a baseball type at all...

Suddenly Jeff wanted to talk to him. Tucking his ball under his arm, he started forwards at a slow run. But as he got closer, he saw Henry turn, and look back down the path he had just walked up. He waited as a tall boy Jeff didn't know caught up with him.

Jeff stopped in his tracks. He didn't feel like going up to Henry if Henry had a friend with him. Jeff walked back to his nice thick tree. And gave it a good pounding...

Soon after that Minna wet herself, and they had to come home.

As it turned out, the trip to the park – and nearly talking to Henry – was the highlight of the weekend. Otherwise it was a bit of a wash-out...

Jeff re-read his old football magazines.

Then he played with his computer game.

Then he stared into space for a bit.

Then he re-read his old football magazines again.

Then he did some more staring.

Finally he started colouring in the headlines on a football magazine front cover. He did it very neatly, without going over any of the lines. But there was nothing to fill in on "Hull City", so the page looked all out of balance...

Mum stuck her head into his room after she put Minna down.

"Hi, Jeff. Want to do something?"

He looked at her. "Like what?"

"Well…what about a board game?"

He gave her One Of His Looks…

"It wasn't so good this week," said Al.

"I thought it was better," said Ben.

"That giant squid…" said Ryan.

"Eight arms are a lot," said Ben.

"Legs," said Ryan.

"What?"

"Eight legs. Animals have legs."

"They do not!" said Ben. "Monkeys have arms!"

"Funny when that guy hit the wreck!" said Al.

"Yeah!" Ben grinned. "We all shouted 'loser!'"

"His face!" Ryan gloated.

"I don't think that tall boy should have won," said Al.

Ryan looked at him. "He didn't."

"Oh," said Al.

Ben turned to Jeff. "What do you think, Jeff? Who do you think should have won?"

Jeff looked back at him. "I don't know."

The three exchanged glances.

"Tuesday at five." Ryan spoke slowly, as if he was talking to someone really stupid. "Every Tuesday at five."

Ben frowned. "Seventeen hours GMT."

"We're still on summer time," said Ryan.

"Fifteen hours GMT, then," said Ben.

"No," said Ryan. "It's either sixteen or eighteen hours GMT."

"Or fourteen hours GMT," said Ben.

Ryan looked sternly at Jeff. "Anyway, it's Tuesday at five."

"Couldn't you just...um, tell me about it?" said Jeff.

There was silence.

Ryan frowned. "It'd take too long to explain."

"You really have to see it," said Ben.

"It's unreal!" said Ryan.

"Yes," agreed Ben. "It's really unreal."

"And it's really real too," said Al.

Jeff gave a sigh.

Suddenly he really missed Dan. Dan would have explained *Cybernauts* to him. He knew he would have. Dan once spent ages telling him the whole plot of a film he had seen on television. (He even acted out the best bits – such as what happened when the big bloke came to the rescue, and how he looked just before he was hit by the axe. And how he looked just after.)

But Dan wasn't here any more. He was hundreds – or was it thousands? – of miles away in America. And Ryan and Ben and Al were all he had.

"Parastinky!"

"Mum, I need some more stationery."
Stationery was good.

"More stationery?"

"Yes. For school."

"Can't we get it on Saturday?"

"No, I need it tonight."

"*Tonight?*"

"Yes. It's for a...geography project."
Geography was likely – you always needed
peculiar stuff for geography.

"Oh."

"Please, Mum."

The stationery shop was just across from
the telly shop. Or rather the telly shop was
just across from the stationery shop. He
wouldn't get the sound, of course, but it was
better than nothing. It was just a question of

getting the timing right...

"There you go!" The salesgirl smiled as she handed Jeff his bag of stationery (some coloured pencils, some felt-tips and a blue bendy thing – he thought he'd better make it look good).

Jeff grabbed the bag from her, and dashed for the exit.

"Jeff, wait!" called Mum, behind him. "Why are you rushing?"

"DEFF!" shouted Minna from her buggy.

"Just gotta..." he shouted back.

He dodged past the crowds at the magazine racks, his eyes straining to see over the busy mall. Yup, there was the television shop, and there were *banks* of tellies – glowing in the window. His heart leapt. He looked at his watch as he ran. Bang on time.

Jeff stopped short in front of the display window.

Yup, there were tellies all right. And the tellies were on. All showing the same thing. But it wasn't *Cybernauts* they were all showing. Oh no. *Cybernauts* it was not. He knew what programme it was, though. He recognised that yellow sofa and the silly-looking bath. *Home Makeover*!

"I liked the T. Rex!" said Al. For some reason he was air-drumming. One of his pretend drums was quite a reach.

"I can't think why that boy went for the pleiosaurs," said Ben. "They aren't dangerous."

"And look what happened to him!" Ryan grinned. "Stuck several billion years ago in time!"

"I felt a bit sorry for him." Al might have been on an imaginary snare drum. Or again he might not. "He looked quite scared. As if it was for real."

"Loser!" said Ryan.

Al gave a little riff in Jeff's direction. "Caught up with it yet, Jeff?"

"Um...no."

Al stopped air-drumming.

The other two looked at him.

"*Still* not watching it?"

"What else do you do on Tuesday evenings?"

Ryan gave a laugh. "He plays with his little sister!"

"I do not!" said Jeff indignantly.

"He plays with himself!"

"I do not!" said Jeff even more indignantly.

"Well, then, why aren't you watching *Cybernauts*?"

"Well…we've got a bit of a problem with the telly at the moment."

The weekend came round again. As weekends do. Suddenly Mum was in a foul mood. Something to do with the state of the world and the environment (she had heard it on the radio). Also the state of Jeff's room, and the mud on the hall carpet (she could see that for herself).

It was Jeff in the firing line.

He started on his room.

But Jeff never found tidying his room an interesting thing to do.

Staring into space was much more interesting.

Perhaps he needed a biscuit…

35

Mum caught him opening a new packet.

"*Don't* open a new packet, when there are biscuits in the biscuit barrel!"

"I don't like the biscuits in the biscuit barrel!"

"They're the same biscuits!" said Mum.

"They're not the same biscuits!"

"They *are* the same biscuits!"

"They're not! They're in the biscuit barrel."

Mum put her hand to her head. "I don't think I'm in the mood for this."

"I don't think I am either," said Jeff.

Mum dumped the barrel in front of him. "IN! THERE!"

Jeff threw the biscuits crossly into the biscuit barrel. (Ha! He bet Ryan's family didn't even have such a stupid thing as a biscuit barrel.)

What was up with Mum anyway?

She had been a lot nicer when they had television.

Or maybe Mum was *always* this bad-tempered, but he had never noticed because he was busy watching the box?

Jeff banged the top back on the biscuit

barrel. Mum and her bad temper were now somewhere else, so he decided to stay in the kitchen.

He sat down at the table, and picked up a pear from the fruit-bowl. He started whirling it around to see how strong the stalk was. It was quite strong. He counted to twenty-four before the pear fell off. He picked it up from the floor, and put it back in the bowl.

Then he did some staring. Then he picked up the label that had come off his new shin-pads. He read the English part. If he wanted to protect his shin-guards from fading, he read, he had to keep them out of direct UV-rays and fluorescent light. Then he started reading what shin-guards were in other languages. Apparently the French for shin-guards was "protége-tibias" and the Spanish was "espinilleras". But Jeff's favourite was the Italian. That was "parastinchi".

He got up and went for the door.

Just then Mum came in. "I'm coming up to look at your room in a minute!" she said. "And if you've just chucked everything under the bed, you'll have to do it again!"

"Parastinky!" muttered Jeff under his breath.

"What?" said Mum dangerously. "*What* did you say?"

"I just said parastinchi!" said Jeff.

Mum narrowed her eyes. "And just what does that mean?"

Jeff tossed his head. "It just happens to be Italian for shin-pads." And he walked out of the kitchen.

Grumping for England

"Have you done your homework?"

Jeff sighed.

"Have you done your *homework?*"

Jeff sighed again.

"Have you done your homework?"

Jeff stopped sighing, and started shouting instead. "WELL, OF COURSE I'VE DONE MY HOMEWORK! THERE'S NOT MUCH ELSE TO DO, IS THERE?!?"

Mum smiled. "OK, then. I'll get Minna ready."

"Ready? What for?"

"Going out."

"Going out?" said Jeff. "Where?"

"The library."

"The library?" cried Jeff. "Why would we want to go to the library? We never go to the

library! None of my friends ever go to the library! Just because we haven't got a telly doesn't mean we have to go to the library! I *won't* go to the library!"

Jeff sat at a table in the library.

He had grumped all the way there. But now he'd arrived, he was still grumping. Hey, he could grump for England! Great Britain. Europe, even!

He scowled around him. He scowled at the books. He scowled at the grey-haired librarian at the check-out desk. He scowled round at the other sad types using the library. Surely the only people who came to the library after the age of about five were losers and anoraks? Or bookish types, like Henry.

He noticed a boy in a woolly hat who was slowly spinning a carousel. He didn't look like an anorak or a loser. In fact he looked all right. But, Jeff supposed, you never could tell.

"Baba!" cried Minna, over in the toddlers' section. She was reading with Mum, and had clearly found a book that hit the spot.

"Baba in cot! Look, baba in cot."

She turned a page, to find an even more exciting picture. "Baba got socks! Baba got socks on!" She was enchanted.

"Sssh," said Mum.

But the librarian didn't seem too bothered. Jeff thought about that. It seemed that you could make a noise in the library as long as you were being enthusiastic. Minna was certainly being enthusiastic.

He, however, was quiet – but unenthusiastic.

He glanced down at some books someone had left on his table. One was about Kalahari bushmen. That figured – libraries always had books about Kalahari bushmen. He flicked through the pages, stopping at a picture of a bushman dad teaching his son to shoot with a bow and arrow. The boy was looking up at his dad happily.

Jeff sighed and picked up a book called *Science for Real – Cool Stuff to Make and Do!*

Hah! he thought. "Cool Stuff" indeed! It was just grown-ups trying to persuade you to learn science. Well, they weren't going to fool him!

He opened the book. Tchah! Making rockets with lemonade bottles. Probably just a model, and it wouldn't actually *go* anywhere. He squinted at the text. It seemed the rocket did go up – quite high in fact. Jeff got a little bit interested, despite himself. And they had nearly finished a big lemonade bottle…

Jeff turned over the page smartly. A hot air balloon. Hmmm. And, before he knew it, he was reading…

Suddenly he realised he'd dropped his grumpy look. He put it on again double-quick, just in case Mum looked over.

After a bit he put away *Science for Real* and turned to another book. This one was about computers. He sighed. Well, why not? There was nothing else to do.

He opened it, and started reading. The first chapter was all about binary numbers. Jeff decided he was not interested in binary numbers. If numbers wanted to be binary, that was fine by him. But couldn't they do it without involving him?

But then he looked at a chart of

conversions, and decided that binary numbers were slightly interesting. It *was* odd, having only "0"s and "1"s. He checked Minna's age in binary code – she was 10, and next birthday would be 11. The birthday after that she would be 100. Then Jeff worked out his own age (he was over 10,000). He started doing Mum's age, but gave up after a bit.

"Nana!" shouted Minna happily. "Baba dot nana!" Clearly this was a thrilling new development.

Jeff flicked on a few pages. Big mistake. He found himself looking at a page of computer graphics. And computer graphics reminded him of…

He glanced at the library clock. Three minutes past five. *Cybernauts* would have just begun. He didn't have to work at the grumpy face now.

Jeff sighed. He could just see them – Ryan, Al and Ben sitting at home in front of their tellies.

There they'd be *goggling* at state-of-the-art graphics, *thrilling* at state-of-the-art battles, *laughing* at state-of-the-art jokes. And shouting

43

"Loser!" when people lost.

And here he was, reading dog-eared books under yellowy lights in the public library.

Jeff sighed again. All his mates – probably his whole class – even Henry would be...

He looked around the library. It was worse than that even. The boy in the woolly hat had gone. There was no one his age in the library at all. There was only a handful of people there. And they were all tinies or adults. And he knew where all the people his age were.

He sat back, aghast. It was terrible.

He was alone, cut off from his generation. He was – let's face it – right out of it. Outside a common culture. He might as well be a Kalahari bushman.

He put his head in his hands. It wasn't just for now, either. Oh, no. Even when he was really old, even when he was sixty, people would still be talking about *Cybernauts*, saying how marvellous it was, and weren't those robot things scary – and he wouldn't have a clue what they were talking about...

Jeff shut his eyes, and leant back in his

chair. Then he leant to one side of his chair, eyes closed.

Then he leant to the other side of his chair, eyes closed.

Then he opened his eyes – and saw the girl.

He straightened up, and moved his chair to get a better look.

The girl was sitting at a table in an alcove. And...and, yes! She was about his own age...

He studied her. Her head was bent over some books, but he could see a bit. She had brown hair and...an ordinary sort of face. A schoolgirl-on-the-bus sort of face. Suddenly the girl tossed her hair back. That was all. But somehow Jeff decided that the girl wasn't quite as ordinary as all that. There was a glint in the eye...

So why wasn't she watching *Cybernauts? Why?*

All at once he had an overwhelming urge to ask her. Before he knew it he was on his feet. A few strides, and he had reached the alcove, and then he was standing at her table.

She looked up, surprised.

"Don't you...don't you...?" Jeff started. The girl's eyebrows rose. Jeff shook his head desperately. "What I mean is, don't you watch *Cybernauts*?"

The girl stared at him for a few seconds. And then she opened her mouth.

She said something, certainly.

She was certainly speaking.

But what it sounded like was this: "Flug wockly boggles!"

Jeff gasped – and backed away. So he had his answer. He knew now why she wasn't watching *Cybernauts*.

She wasn't watching *Cybernauts* because she was foreign. Or an alien. Or...

"Potty!" cried Minna from the other side of the library.

"Yup!" thought Jeff to himself. "Or that!"

Eight Queens

One evening Mum got out the old chess set.

"Knight next to the castle," said Mum as they were setting up.

"I *know*!" said Jeff.

"Queen on her own colour."

"Oh. Yes."

At least it was a fairly fast game. Jeff hated slow chess.

At one point he took Mum's queen. But Mum fought back pretty hard...

"Don't chew the chessmen," said Mum, while he was pondering.

"It's not a chessman. It's your queen."

"It's still a chessman, and don't chew her!"

"I wasn't chewing her, I was sucking her!"

"Well, please don't suck my queen!"

In the end Mum won. "You opened yourself

up on your diagonals," she said, clearing away the pieces.

"Oh. Did I?"

"Yes. Do you want another game?"

"*No.*"

"OK, then. I'll set you a little *problemo.*"

"A what?"

"A little chess *problemo.*"

"I don't want a little chess *problemo*!"

"Yes, you do." Mum piled eight black pawns onto the board, and said. "Pretend these are all queens!"

"Why?"

"Just pretend! Now put them all on the board so they are not in line with any other pawn, I mean, queen. And that includes diagonals."

"Eight of them?" Jeff placed a few pawns round the board, and frowned. "It's not possible."

"Isn't it?"

"Well, is it?"

"I'm not telling."

"Humph!" Jeff moved some pawns around

48

the board for a few minutes, but then said, "I give up."

"Don't give up." Mum got to her feet.

"Why not?"

"Because it's fun," said Mum over her shoulder, as she walked out.

Fun? *Fun?* FUN?

Fun was watching rubbish TV! Not doing Mum's little chess problemo!

Jeff knelt on top of the wall, panting. Then he looked down the garden.

Yes, there it was. The square of light flickered in the house beyond. It was getting dark now, but the curtains still hadn't been drawn.

Slowly Jeff edged along the wall. The brick was damp after the rain. His hands were cold, and he could feel the wet seeping through his jeans at the knees. He shivered – and crawled on…

He hadn't really meant to do this.

It all started when he looked out of his window – and saw the telly on in the house backing onto theirs. It had taken about fifteen seconds – including a time-check – to get from his room to the wall.

And here he was, crawling through the cold wintry dusk towards...*Cybernauts*! (It had to be *Cybernauts* on that telly. Had to be. There were kids in that house. Jeff had heard them. And if there were kids...)

He came to a bush, which grew over the wall from Mr Rigby's side. He rose to a crouching position, and made his way gingerly over the dark wet leaves.

He glanced up again. The flickering square was bigger now. And he could make out shapes. A sort of rocket thing zoomed from one corner, making the whole screen yellow. That could be it. That could be *Cybernauts*. *Surely* it was *Cybernauts*.

Jeff's heart leapt. Now if he got down to the bottom wall, he would really get quite a good view. He wouldn't hear anything, of course, but at least he would be able to see...

He took a step forward.

And then it happened.

Suddenly the evening air was rent by a loud

blood-curdling yowl.

"Miiiiiiiaaaaaaooooooooowww!!!"

This was followed by a loud blood-curdling hiss.

"Hssssssttttt!!!"

"A cat," thought Jeff to himself.

And he was half-right.

The first cat never even saw Jeff. It ran full-pelt along the wall, and crashed straight into his legs.

Before Jeff could do anything, it wriggled away and jumped sideways into the garden. The second cat leapt after it, and they both streaked away into the dusk.

The cats were back on course.

Jeff wasn't.

He was wobbling.

He was wobbling badly.

He was going to fall! No, he wasn't! Yes, he was! No, he wasn't! Ye…

He fell.

The wrong side of the wall.

There was a crack and a thump.

*

Jeff looked around. His back hurt. He was winded. And he seemed to be lying on a plastic box-thing, the sort you keep plants in. Yes, that was it. Except this box-thing was bust. And the plants weren't in it. They were out of it. All over the place. And there was earth everywhere…

Suddenly there was more light, and he heard a door open.

"What the…" It was Mr Rigby's voice. Footsteps – then an anguished wail.

"My Horti-box! My hyacinths!"

Mr Rigby's head appeared over him. "You!" he cried. "So it's you, is it?"

Jeff gazed up at the thin, angry face and wondered. Was it him? Was he him? Or was he someone else?

"What do you mean by crashing into my garden? Wrecking my Horti-box?"

Mr Rigby's voice rose higher with each question. "What were you doing?"

Jeff frowned. What had he been doing? He considered.

Slowly the answer took shape in his

mind, slowly the words came, slowly he drew breath.

"I was just trying to watch television," he said.

"Dah-dah-der-*dah*!" Ryan was singing something under his breath.

Then Ben joined in. "Der-der-dah!"

Then Al joined in. At least Jeff thought he was joining in. He may have been singing something quite different. Al did not have perfect pitch.

Ryan stopped singing, and frowned. "It wasn't that good last night. Those slugs!"

"The weird thing with two heads was OK," said Ben.

"It wasn't two heads," said Al. "It was two eyes."

Ryan looked at him. "Think about it, Al."

Al nodded. "Two eyes. Weird!"

"That girl was quite a good pilot," said Ben.

Ryan shook his head. "Nah! Girls can't pilot!"

"How difficult do you think it is?" said Al.

"Not that difficult," said Ryan.

"Quite difficult," said Ben.

"Depends what you mean by 'difficult'," said Ryan.

Al looked at him. "Not...easy."

"I know what 'difficult' means, you drop-kick!" said Ryan.

"Oh."

"You know what?" Ryan said slowly. "There's only one way to find out how difficult it is."

"How?" said Ben.

"Go on it."

"Hey!" Ben's eyes lit up. "Cool idea!"

"Do you think we could?" said Al.

"Of course!" said Ryan. "We'd be better than some of those losers!"

"I suppose we write in," said Ben.

"I'll find the address," said Al.

"I'd like to meet Baz Haskins," said Ryan.

Everyone fell about.

"Baz Haskins!" cried Ben.

"Baz Haskins!" cried Ryan.

"Baz Haskins!" cried Al.

Jeff decided to risk a question. "Who's Baz

Haskins?"

There was a silence.

"Oh, he's...Baz Haskins!" said Ben.

"He's the guy who...er..."

"Does it!"

"Er...does what?" said Jeff.

"*Cybernauts*, you dope!"

Man and Machine

"The steam engine was first used to pump water from mines," Mr Dawson said, pointing to the picture on the whiteboard. "Later it became the driving force of the entire industrial process."

He threw his pen in the air and caught it again. If this was aimed at getting better attention, it didn't work. He could probably have juggled five pens and an automatic pencil sharpener without waking anyone up.

No one was concentrating. Even Henry, Jeff saw, was gazing out of the window.

History was usually better than this.

There were boring teachers in Jeff's school.

There were *very* boring teachers in Jeff's school.

But Mr Dawson wasn't one of them.

Sometimes they had good laughs in history. But now they had got on to the Industrial Revolution, and the fizz had gone out of things.

Jeff doodled down the side of his pad. He was trying to write his name in three-dimensional blocks, but he couldn't quite work out which bits to shade. The F's were particularly difficult.

Dawson was making sort of summing-up noises now.

Maybe he should listen.

On the other hand he was just getting the shading on his F's right...

Suddenly his hand stopped. What was that old Dawson was saying? Television? Had he heard right? Jeff was pretty sure that the television was not an Industrial Revolution invention. Cathode rays and stuff came later, surely. So why was Dawson on about it?

Jeff looked up to see Dawson writing on the whiteboard. *Man and Machine: The Industrial Revolution*. Followed by a date, a time and a channel. A *TV* channel.

"I strongly suggest you watch this," their teacher was saying. "It should be good – bring the whole subject alive for you."

Some of the girls started making, "Yes, of course we will!" and "How very interesting!" noises.

"And we'll kick off next lesson with a discussion of the programme," Dawson finished. And then the bell went.

Jeff did not stampede off with the rest. He collected his stuff up slowly, and sidled up to Mr Dawson, who was putting some papers into a folder.

"Er...Mr Dawson."

"Yes, Jeff?" Mr Dawson looked at him over his half-moon glasses.

"That programme on the Industrial Revolution you were talking about..."

"Yes?"

"Well, it sounds very interesting."

"Good, good!" Mr Dawson went on shuffling papers into his folder.

Jeff hunched his shoulders. "But I'm awfully sorry, I can't watch it."

"Ah, well." Mr Dawson popped the button on his folder shut. "Perhaps you could video it."

"No, we can't do that either. You see...we don't have a television."

Mr Dawson did not look astounded. Nor did he bark, "No television? You poor deprived child!" He just looked mildly interested. "Oh?"

Jeff heaved a big sigh. "My mum got rid of it."

Dawson raised an eyebrow. "And why was that?"

"Because she's mean," is what Jeff would have *liked* to have said. But he didn't say that. "She said we were watching too much."

Dawson seemed more interested now.

Jeff pressed on. "So perhaps you could tell her at Parents' Evening that we must get one again, so I can watch educational stuff." He gave another little sigh. "After all, I don't want to get behind-hand."

Mr Dawson gave a roar. Jeff flinched. But it turned out to be a roar of approval. Not for Jeff, and his serious attitude towards

59

schoolwork. But for Mum. "Got rid of the television, has she? Splendid stuff! That's what I like to hear! I wish we had more parents like yours, Jeff!"

"So you...won't speak to her at Parents' Evening?"

"Indeed I shall! I shall congratulate her!"

"But...but what about this programme on the Industrial Revolution?"

Mr Dawson waved a hand. "Oh, never mind about that! I just wanted you lot to switch over from your usual mindless junk!" He closed his folder, tucked it under his arm, and made for the door. As he left the room, he called back over his shoulder. "Read some books, boy! Books! That's the stuff! And tell me what you find out about the Luddites!"

And then he was gone.

Jeff stood in front of the desk for a moment. And then he heard a noise behind him. He swung round. It was Henry.

Jeff stared at him. It was not a good moment. Had Henry been in the classroom the whole time? Had he heard everything? Jeff ran through the conversation with Dawson in his head. He didn't feel he had appeared *quite* his best.

Their eyes met. Jeff thought he ought to say something. "Dawson, eh?"

"Yes," said Henry. "That was definitely Dawson. He teaches us history."

Jeff turned to go, but suddenly a thought struck him. "You know, Henry, I saw you in the park the other day. With a mitt!"

"With a mitt?" Now it was Henry's turn to look taken aback.

"Yes, a baseball mitt!"

"O-oh! A *glove*! Yes, I remember!" Henry grinned. "Entertaining cousins. You know."

Jeff looked at him.

"Not really," he said. And he dashed after the others.

He caught up with Ben, Al and Ryan in the playground. None of them ever waited for him.

Ryan looked at him when he came up. "What were you saying to Dawson? We could hear him bellowing down the corridor."

"Barking, more like!" said Al.

"He is barking," said Ben.

"Oh, it was about that programme he asked us to watch," Jeff explained. "I said I wouldn't be watching."

"Good lad!" said Ryan. "That's the spirit!"

Al looked at Jeff. "Why? Why aren't you going to watch it?"

Suddenly all three were looking at him.

Jeff looked back at them.

This was it.

The million-dollar question.

Jeff couldn't put off telling the truth any longer.

Jeff didn't want to put off telling the truth any longer.

"We don't have a television," he said.

There was dead silence.

"What? Not at all?" said Ryan.

"No."

"You must have one *somewhere*," said Ben.

"Nope!" said Jeff.

"I didn't think it was *possible* not to have a television!"

"Oh, it is."

"*Why?*"

"My mum got rid of it."

There was another silence.

"My mum wouldn't dare do a thing like that," said Ben.

"Mine neither," said Al.

Ryan frowned. "I don't think he handles his mum very well."

"No," agreed Al.

"Mind you," said Ben. "His mum…"

Ben nodded. "She's quite a…"

"Now, hang on!" said Jeff. "She's OK, my mum. But she gets these ideas into her head, and – it's difficult to get them out again…" He trailed off.

Al spoke. "Well, you could always come and watch it at my place."

"Or mine," said Ben.

"Thanks," said Jeff. "But it's too far." Both Al and Ben lived way across town – a bus change. "Mum would never…"

"Tell you what!" said Al. "I'll video it. And then you can come and watch it at the weekend."

"Would you?" said Jeff. "Could I?"

Al nodded. "No problem…"

Ben looked at Jeff and a gleam came into his eye. "Hey, Jeff?"

Jeff looked at him warily. "Yes?"

Ben grinned. "Do you have those lights which go on when you flick a switch?"

Everyone seemed to think that was *so* funny…

News from America

"Al?"

"Mmm?"

"Did you video that programme, Al?"

"Oh!" Al slapped his leg. "Oh, Jeff, I forgot! I'm really sorry!"

"It was good last night," said Ryan.

"I didn't think so," said Ben. "I didn't believe those cyborgs for a second."

"The cyborgs were *good*!" said Al.

Jeff turned and walked away.

That weekend Jeff rang Dan in America. It was good to hear his voice. Cheerful. Dan-ish.

"Tell me about America," said Jeff.

"Well...it's a big country north of—"

"No, not America! *You in* America!"

"Oh, *me in* America. Well, what do you

want to know?"

"Hmm. Let's think. Do you go through a metal-detector to go into school?"

"We used to," said Dan. "But it was vandalised so we don't have it any more."

"And do you have a flag at the corner of your classroom?"

"Yup! And we take the Pledge of Allegiance every morning."

"You do?"

"I know it by heart now. Like a real American. I'll recite it for you if you want. *I pledge allegiance to the Flag—*"

"That's OK! I believe you!" said Jeff.

"OK!" said Dan cheerily. "What else do you want to know?"

"Erm…" Jeff searched around for more questions. For some reason he thought of Henry. Henry and his baseball mitt. "Are you playing any sport? Baseball?"

"Not baseball."

"Not American football?"

"No! I've gone for the hoops."

"*Croquet?*"

Dan laughed. "Not croquet, you dope. Basketball!"

"Right. Basketball." Jeff thought. "I forget. Is basketball a contact sport?"

Dan laughed again. "I don't know, I must ask someone some time."

"So are you good at the hoops?"

"Fantastic!"

"You are?"

"*No!*" said Dan. "The guys here have been playing it for ever."

"Perhaps you'd better be a cheerleader then. I think you'd look cute with those big pom-poms."

"Big pom-poms yourself!" said Dan.

Jeff laughed.

Dan said, "What about you?"

"Me?"

"Yes! What have you been up to?"

A lot of not watching telly.

A lot of staring.

Going to the library...

"Mmmm...nothing much. Usual stuff."

"Who are you hanging with?"

"Well...Ryan and his lot, I suppose."

"Oh, you mean Ryan Fuller. And Al?"

"Yup. And Ben."

"Oh. OK."

There was a second or two of silence.

Jeff decided it was easier to talk about America. "Well, it sounds as though you're having an OK time."

"Yeah." Dan paused. "Different. I miss stuff. Like English chocolate. And baked beans."

"Baked beans?"

"Yes, they're not the same here. They don't make them right."

"Oh dear!" Jeff started laughing. "That's terrible!"

"It is terrible!" said Dan indignantly.

"At least it saves on your problem," said Jeff.

"I do not have a problem," said Dan.

"With baked beans you have a problem."

"With baked beans I do *not* have a problem."

"You're lying. Going to America has made you into a liar!"

"No! Staying in England has made *you* into a liar!"

Jeff grinned at the wall. It was good to talk to Dan.

"And I miss the footie," said Dan.

"Of course you do."

"How's the Big Signing coming on?"

"The Big Signing has injured his big metatarsal."

"Oh."

After a bit of footie chat, Jeff said, "Better go now. G'day, mate!"

"That's Australian, you idiot!" said Dan.

"Oh. What do Americans say when they say goodbye?"

"Goodbye!" said Dan, and rang off laughing.

That evening Mum got out her old tapes, and the three of them danced in the front room. They danced and danced.

"Mum, you are a pretty cool dancer!" said Jeff.

"I am, aren't I?" Mum grinned at him. "And you're not so bad yourself!"

"Do you think?"

Mum nodded. "Perhaps it's in the genes."

They both looked at Minna, waving her fat arms to "Dancing Queen", very out of time.

"Perhaps not," said Mum.

An Evil Plot?

"High fives!" Jeff came dancing into the kitchen.

"OK," said Mum. She turned and did High Fives with him. Then he had to do High Fives with Minna's sticky little hand. Then Mum had to do them with Minna.

"Why?" said Mum, when the High Fives session was over.

"Why what?" said Jeff.

"Why are we high-fiving?"

"Erm...I've forgotten."

"Oh, come on."

"All right, then. I've cracked your little chess *problemo*. The eight queens. It's there, on the board now."

"Hey, fantastic!"

Jeff gave a sigh.

Then Mum said. "Aren't you pleased?"

Jeff sighed again. "Not, really. I'm just sad, that's all."

"Why?"

"Because I've just spent a lot of time doing something that will never be any use at all…"

"You never know," said Mum.

Minna put up her hand to him. "I-Fi's!" she demanded.

Tuesday afternoon came round again. *Cybernauts* time for some. Not for Jeff, though. Once again Jeff was walking up the steps of the library. He could have gone shopping with Mum and Minna. But the library won. Just.

He stomped down the street, up the steps of the library, turned right, and walked through the swing doors of the junior section. He looked around, and took a deep breath. Oh, well – better make the best of it.

He finally found the history section. He chose four books on the Industrial Revolution, and went and sat down at one of the tables. At

first he tried to pile up the books in order o
size, but it didn't work, because of a short
wide one. Then he tried to pile the books in
order of interesting-looking-ness, but he
couldn't choose between the two dullest.
Finally, he opened one of them...

It started with a picture of some cloth-
makers before the Industrial Revolution. The
whole family worked together in one room –
carding, spinning, winding thread, or weaving.
There was a fire burning, and it looked quite
cosy, Jeff thought. In the corner of the room
there was a bucket. This, Jeff read, was used
to collect the family's urine, for sale to the
local fulling mill, where cloth was finished off.
Jeff smiled to himself. Ryan's surname was
Fuller. Somehow he liked the thought of
Ryan's forebears paying a penny a tub for
peoples' wee...

Jeff looked up from his book to see who
else was in the library. There were a few
toddlers again with their mums. But there were
also – over in the corner – two boys. They
were reading Asterix books.

ed at them. Foreign or mad? Or just
t was hard to tell…

He went back to the book. Things changed as he turned the pages. There was a picture of a huge factory floor, covered with looms. Children worked underneath them gathering threads. The mines were even worse. Two boys about his age were shown, hauling huge baskets along narrow tunnels in total darkness.

Jeff leant back in his chair. What was it Dawson had told him to research? Yes, that was it. *Luddites.* He looked through his books until he found a reference. It seemed that Luddites were workers who broke the new machines in protest at the unemployment they caused. After one attack on a mill, they were arrested, and seventeen were hanged…

But, of course, they changed nothing. They were powerless against the onward march of technology. A bit like his Mum, thought Jeff. Wasn't getting rid of the television just setting your face against progress?

Suddenly Jeff thought about the "flug wockly" girl. He glanced towards her table – and stared. The girl was there. At the same table. Sitting there. Just as before. She had a big pile of books in front of her and was writing on a notepad. Concentrating.

Jeff considered her, as she bent over her writing. The memory of what had happened two weeks ago was fresh. Jeff still felt sore.

As he gazed at her, she looked up. *Straight at him.*

He dropped his eyes to his book. And started reading again.

"Minding the new machines was desperately dull work…" He stopped. Reading about it was pretty dull too. He closed the book.

Jeff leant back in his chair and stuck his feet out in front of him.

Then he bent his knees and tried to put the soles of his feet together while still in a sitting position.

Then he tried to put his feet on the floor in a straight line with his heels together.

Then he tried to put his feet on the floor in a straight line with his toes together.

That seemed to be about it for interesting things to do with his legs.

He looked around the library for a fresh challenge...

Ah! There was one of those things with books in that go round and round. He got up, went up to it, and gave it a push. It did go round and round, in a rather wobbly way. What it needed, Jeff thought, was more speed. Jeff gave it more speed. A few pushes, and it was spinning quite well. Probably about 150 r.p.m. Whoosh! Books careered in front of his eyes, to the sound of a sort of trundling noise. Jeff watched happily. Who cared if it disturbed other library-users and "flug wockly" girls? This was literature in the round!

Finally he let it grind to a halt. He watched it come to a complete stop – and found himself looking straight into the eyes of a woman. A woman with purple eyes. She had grey hair too, but it was the purple eyes you noticed. She was on the front cover of a book. He grabbed it, and took it back to his table.

He knew who the woman with purple eyes

was, because Dan had once told him about the book. It was a "wicked" story, Dan had said. Jeff had not taken much notice then, but now that he and Dan were older (and thousands of miles apart), he suddenly wanted to look at Dan's "wicked" story.

He looked at the woman with the purple eyes, and tried to remember what Dan had said. Yes, that was it. She was a mad and evil headmistress, who hypnotised all her pupils. (Dan had done a good impression of a hypnotised pupil walking downstairs, and had nearly fallen on top of Alison Pringle.) Once the mad and evil headmistress had hypnotised everyone in her school, apart from the hero, she got even more mad and evil. At the end, the mad and evil headmistress tried to get on television to hypnotise everyone in the world.

Television, thought Jeff to himself, gazing at the purple eyes. Of course! Television *would* be a good way to hypnotise people – a *great* way to hypnotise people. Especially if it was a really popular programme, like, say, *Cybernauts*.

Yeah...Jeff leant back in his seat. Suppose

77

that was really happening. Suppose this Baz Haskins person and his computer graphics were part of an evil plot to hypnotise people. After all, Mum had said that *he* went into a trance when watching television, and that was ordinary television. Supposing *Cybernauts* took it a step further? Hmmm. He thought about the way his friends went on and on and on about *Cybernauts*. Not natural, was it? Not natural at all...

Suddenly Jeff had a picture of Al, and Ben, and Ryan, all marching around with staring eyes. *Programmed*. And everyone else who watched *Cybernauts* marching around, programmed. Everyone, that is...except him!

Jeff sat up and straightened his shoulders. Yes, he was the one. The one who didn't watch *Cybernauts*. The one who didn't get hypnotised. He was going to *save the world*!

He grinned to himself. Yup, Ben and Ryan and Al would be pretty sick if he saved the world and became a hero through not watching *Cybernauts*!

A thought struck him. He wasn't the only

one, though, was he?

What about the two boys reading Asterix? He looked over – they weren't there any longer.

Well, what about...the "flug wockly boggles" girl?

Was she going to share the glory of saving the world?

He looked towards her table – and got a shock.

The "flug wockly boggles" girl wasn't sitting at her table.

She was standing.

At his table.

And she was about to say something!

He goggled at her.

Then she said it.

"Do you have any change?"

Dizzi

Jeff gaped at her. And thought over what she had said. It sounded like English. Very like English.

The girl held out her hand towards him. She was holding a fifty pence piece.

"Do you have any change?" she repeated. "I need it for the photocopier."

Finally Jeff found his voice. "You're English?"

The girl nodded. "Yes."

"You speak English?"

She nodded again. "Yes."

"You've been English all this time?"

The girl looked a bit puzzled, but nodded for a third time. "Yes."

Indignation welled up inside him. When he had *needed* an English person about his age to prove that English people about his age were not watching *Cybernauts*, she could have done it. But she didn't, did she? She had let him down. Tricked him. "Well, why did you pretend to be foreign?" he demanded.

The girl looked at him, surprised. "Did I?"

"Yes! You did! You talked all funny. You said – you said all that fluck woggly stuff."

The girl gave a little gasp. "Oh, yes. I remember now. That was you, was it?"

"Yes," said Jeff. "It was."

"Oh."

"Well, why did you do it?"

The girl thought for a moment. Then she said, "It was performance art."

"*What?*"

"Performance art. You can go around doing silly things if it's performance art, and everyone thinks it's wonderful."

"Well, I didn't think it was wonderful!" snapped Jeff.

"Oh," said the girl lightly. "You were one of my failures, then."

Jeff grunted, and picked his book up again.

"*OK*," said the girl, in a sudden change of tone.

Jeff looked at her. "OK, what?"

She met his eye. "It wasn't performance art. I was just being...a bit stupid."

All at once Jeff relaxed. He approved of people who admitted they had been stupid. There seemed to be very few of them around.

"You see..." The girl frowned, trying to remember. "I was writing this letter to the council about bike parking, and I was just getting to the good bit, and I didn't want to be interrupted. It was a spur-of-the-moment thing."

"Oh."

"As I say, a bit...stupid." The girl looked at him and grinned. "Though you should have seen your..." She broke off.

"Should have seen my what?" said Jeff crossly.

"Um...oh, nothing." The girl waved a hand vaguely in the air, then met his eye. "Well, do you have any change?"

Jeff shook his head. He had no money at all

since paying for Mr Rigby's Horti-box. But he wasn't going to explain that to her.

"OK." The girl started to turn away, but then she seemed to change her mind. She looked at him with interest.

"That time..."

"Yes?" said Jeff.

"When you came up to me..."

"Yes?" said Jeff.

"Why were you asking about *Cybernauts*?"

There was silence.

Finally Jeff sighed. "It's a long story."

The girl's eyes narrowed.

It was five minutes later.

Jeff was sitting at the girl's table (as it was more out of the way), and he was telling her the "long story".

But he had decided to make it more dramatic. "In fact it's not that interesting inside a telly. Just wires and...er, stuff. And after Mum finished with the axe, she threw the whole thing in the bin. And jumped on it."

The girl – who had told him she was called

Dizzi – looked impressed. "Just like that? With no explanation?"

"No." Jeff shook his head. "Completely off the wall. She just lost it."

"Goodness! But surely something triggered it!"

Jeff considered. "Maybe it was because they took off her favourite programme."

"Her favourite programme?"

"Yup."

"So what was that? A soap or something?"

"No." Jeff shook his head. "*Home Makeover.*"

"Wow!" Dizzi stared at him with her big brown eyes. "Does she often get like that?"

"Not often, no." Jeff felt a twinge of guilt. But he was only getting his own back, he told himself. For "flug wockly boggles".

Suddenly Dizzi brightened. "I know! I'll write to the telly people and ask them to put *Home Makeover* back on!"

Jeff shook his head sadly. "Too late," he said. "Our telly is beyond repair."

Dizzi looked thoughtful. "It must be odd

without a telly."

"It is."

"I guess I'd miss it."

"You would."

"Mind you, I wouldn't be that bothered about *Cybernauts*."

He looked at her. "Wouldn't you?"

"No, it's a...*kid's* programme. The computer graphics are great, OK. But it's really just kids doing computer games!"

"Is that all?"

"Just about."

Jeff sighed. "My friends go on and on and on about it!"

Dizzi wrinkled her nose. "Sound dead boring, your friends."

Jeff was silent. *Dead boring*. He didn't know whether to be offended or to agree with her. Instead he said, "In fact they go on so much about it, that I – that *another* friend – thinks it's a bit sinister. He has a theory about it."

"Oh, yes?"

Jeff explained his hypnotism-by-television-leading-to-world-domination theory. As he finished, he glanced at Dizzi to see her grinning at him.

"Your friend watches too much telly!" she said.

"He doesn't!"

"He does!"

"Why?"

"That guy, that Baz Haskins – he couldn't hypnotise anyone!"

"Couldn't he? Why not?"

Dizzi thought. "His hair."

"*His hair?*"

She nodded. "You couldn't hypnotise anyone with that hair. It's not possible. They'd just start laughing."

"Oh," said Jeff.

There was a short silence.

"What's wrong with his hair?" said Jeff.

"Well, it's—" Dizzi stopped, and shook her head. "No, I can't explain. You just have to see for yourself."

Jeff sighed. "Everyone says that, and I can't. People say they'll video it and stuff, but so far I haven't seen *one* single second of *one* single episode."

"You know," said Dizzi slowly. "It'd be fun to see someone you know on *Cybernauts*."

"I'd just like to see it," said Jeff.

Dizzi looked dreamy. "Someone you *know* piloting those spaceships and fighting those battles."

"Getting to watch one episode," said Jeff. "That would suit me fine."

"Someone who…" Dizzi trailed off, her eyes fixed on him. *"Yes!"*

"Yes, what?" said Jeff.

"I've had an idea, Jeff!"

"What?" said Jeff.

"What's my idea? Well, it's…" She broke off. "I tell you what, I'll video *Cybernauts* for you, and the next time you go somewhere where they've got a video, you can play it! OK?"

"Er…OK."

"Great. Just give me your address, will you?"

"Who was that you were talking to?" said Mum, as she lowered the buggy down

87

the library steps.

"Oh...no one," said Jeff.

"She's not at your school, is she?" said Mum.

"No," said Jeff.

The buggy landed on the pavement with a bump. Minna slept on. Jeff felt the cold wind in his face, as they started up the road.

"It's just when I came in and waved at you just now, she gave me this strange look."

"Did she?"

"Yes. A *really* strange look."

Jeff pulled up his collar and buttoned his jacket. "Can't think why," he said. "No, I really can't think why she did that..."

"Zippitty-doo-dah!"

"You're supposed to go *down* the slide, Minna!"

But it was no good.

Minna gritted her teeth, held on to the sides and inched her way up the slide. Her rubber-soled shoes squeaked on the shiny surface.

Jeff watched her. Why did she have to be so different? Wasn't it easier to do what everyone else did? It was a good thing it was getting late, and there were so few kids in the playground.

Minna had to pause for breath twice, but she finally made it to the top. She stood triumphantly on top of the slide, surveying the playground. Then she climbed down the steps, and made for the sandpit.

There was a smell of autumn in the air. Jeff wandered over to the big play-frame. He looked at the six chains hanging on the horizontal wooden beam. You swung from one side to another. At least you did, if you were fit. Jeff had never managed it. It was very sore on the hands.

Jeff turned to look at Minna.

Then he looked back at the chains.

Then he looked at Minna.

Then he looked back at the chains.

Then he leapt.

He knew to use the impetus from the initial leap to swing to the second chain, and then the third. This was when he usually fell off.

But for some reason he was determined to get further this time. Speed was the thing, he knew that. The longer the pain took to register on his hands and arms, the better. He kicked with his legs to give his body swing, and lunged for the fourth chain. He caught it, transferred his weight, and grabbed the fifth. Then a wild swipe. He thought he wasn't going to make it.

But somehow he caught the sixth chain, pulled himself on to it with an arm-wrenching jerk, hung from it for a split second – then dropped to the rubberised ground.

Result!

"You've lost weight!" said Mum, walking round the side of the play-frame with her shopping.

He looked at her, panting. "Have I?"

Minna came up, trailing sand.

"Yup!" said Mum. "I reckon it's because of the telly."

"What?" His heart was still hammering.

"All that television you used to watch. Made you fat."

"I wasn't fat."

"No. But that friend of yours is a bit fat."

"Ryan?"

"Yes. I wouldn't want Ryan sitting on my head."

"I wouldn't want Ryan sitting on my head either."

"Sit on *'is* 'ead!" said Minna fiercely.

"I had no idea!" Ryan said, as they collected by the science block wall.

"Me neither!" said Ben.

"They might have said something," said Al.

"They ought to warn you," said Ryan.

"I think television people have a *responsibility*," said Ben.

"Just taking it off like that!" said Ryan.

"They might have said something," said Al.

Jeff looked at them. "Not…what…you mean *Cybernauts*?"

"Yes, *Cybernauts*!" snapped Ryan.

"Over," said Al.

"Out," said Ben.

"Off," said Ryan.

"Over and out and off," said Ben.

"End of the series," said Ryan.

"A very short series," said Al.

"A pilot," said Ben.

"A very long pilot," said Al.

For a few seconds Jeff just stood there. Then he opened his mouth and went, "****! ****! ******!"

A bunch of girls across the way looked at him with disapproval, and the blonde one giggled, but he couldn't care less…

＊

Later, as he was stabbing holes in his eraser in maths, he thought about it. Maybe *Cybernauts* going off *wasn't* such bad news. OK, now he was never going to have a chance to see the thing. He'd never ever be able to join in a *Cybernauts* conversation. But maybe now his friends would stop going on about it.

Suddenly he thought of Dizzi. He reckoned he'd probably heard the last of Dizzi. She had his address, but there was no video to send now, was there? No. He had certainly heard the last of Dizzi…

He stomped home in a bad mood.

And found an envelope.

An envelope addressed to him.

An envelope addressed to him in big round confident writing.

It wasn't Dan's writing. In fact it didn't look like a boy's writing at all.

Jeff opened the envelope and pulled out a white postcard, decorated with a shower of stickers. One was a glorious star-burst of pink and orange. It said, "Zippitty-doo-dah!" He turned it over to see the signature. "Dizzi."

Dizzi had had to fit in the writing between the stickers.

"Hi, Jeff," he read. "I was all set with my zapper, but *Cybernauts* has been pulled. *Cyber-knickers!*" This was followed by a lot of exclamation marks. "There was some ridiculous American thing – you would not *believe* what the girls were wearing! But why not meet up you-know-where??? (I mean the library.) Same day! Same time! Same table! (I'm usually there Tuesdays, because my dad works in the music section.)"

She finished, "Your new (and deeply cool) friend, Dizzi!"

Right at the bottom, she added, "PS: You were having me on about the axe and jumping in the bin, weren't you?"

Jeff grinned, and stuffed the card into his pocket.

Deeply cool, hmmm.

So that was why she was always there on Tuesdays.

Tuesdays, hmmm.

Well, he'd have finished most of his books by Tuesday. And he wasn't going to finish that fantasy anyway. He didn't believe one word of it.

New friend, hmmm.

He sauntered through the swing doors, and glanced around.

The library was busier than usual. But Dizzi was not at her table. He carried his books over to the check-in.

It took some time as the girl in front of him was complaining about a tape she had borrowed. She was about his age, and she was good at complaining. At one point she gave a demonstration of what the last tape in the box had sounded like. *"Neee-aw-eeeeh-oh!"* As the tape was ruined, she said, she never found out the end of the story, and whether the nice conman was the hero's father or not. On the whole she thought he probably was. The librarian told the girl she could get another tape out for free.

When Jeff had checked in his books, he wandered down the middle aisle, looking around him. No, not a sign of Dizzi. There were two girls about her age, but they were in a maroon school uniform.

Then suddenly he spotted someone, half-hidden by a table, kneeling on the floor at the non-fiction section. He craned his neck for a better view. He – or she – was kneeling by the bottom shelf, nose in a book. Yes, it was a girl, and yes…it *was* Dizzi! Jeff's heart leapt.

He walked closer, and was just about to hiss "Dizzi!" when suddenly he stopped. It was certainly Dizzi, but her head looked different. Well, not so much her head, more her hair. She had put her hair in bunches! Tied with loopy silver ribbon. Lots of loopy silver ribbon!

Jeff hesitated.

He wasn't quite sure about loopy silver bunches.

He didn't know where he *was* with a girl in loopy silver bunches.

Suppose someone he knew saw him *talking* to a girl in loopy silver bunches?

He started walking slowly past behind her.

And at that moment Dizzi looked up from her book. "Hi there, Jeff!" she said. And she grinned.

He looked down at her. And suddenly found himself grinning back...

The World Champion

Half-term was a problem. What to do? *Not a lot*, was Jeff's solution to the problem. He made a dragster with CDs for wheels from a kit Mum bought him. And they all went to the cinema. But time still hung heavy. You can stare into space for so long. But then you have to do something else. Jeff invented a new sport.

It was a sport of two parts. First Jeff kicked his football towards the end of the garden. Then he shot an arrow from his old bow to see if he could hit it. Hitting the football was good but making it move was even better. Triple points (Jeff later changed it to quadruple points). One good thing about the new sport was that the arrow went low, so there was virtually no chance of it going over the wall (Jeff didn't want any more grief from Mr Rigby).

"I've invented a new sport," he told Mum when she came out.

"Good," said Mum.

"I'm the British champion."

"Excellent!"

"World champion, in fact."

"Congratulations!"

"Well, only because it's just been invented," he added modestly.

"I see." Mum bent down, and started pulling up some weeds. "Just make sure Minna's not in the garden, though, won't you? I know those arrows aren't sharp, but even so."

"Sure, Mum."

"So what are you going to call it?"

"What?"

"This sport you're the world champion of? It ought to have a name."

"Hmmm." He thought. "Well...it's a mixture of football and archery, but starts with football and has a lot more of archery in it..."

"So?"

"I'm going to call it Farchery."

The letter came on a Saturday. Jeff was eating his breakfast.

"Something for you, Jeff!" Mum chucked an envelope across the table.

Jeff caught it just before it fell into his cereal. It was an official-looking typed letter. No stamp. Instead it was franked with the letters, "CaD-TV".

Carefully he opened it.

"My letter!" wailed Minna. "Wan' my letter!"

"All right, Minna," said Mum. "You can have one too." And she stuffed a bill back into a brown envelope. "Here you are!"

Minna beamed as she took it. "*My* letter, Deff! Dis my letter!"

Jeff began reading his letter.

"Dear Jeff Wilson," it said. "Following the outstanding success of the last series of *Cybernauts*, a new series is shortly to go into production…"

He frowned. OK, that was interesting,

perhaps, but why write to him?

"Your name has been put forward…"

He blinked, and the letters seemed to jump all over the place.

"…as a possible contestant."

He yelped.

Minna, who was reading her letter, yelped too.

Mum was looking at him. Silently he handed her the letter. She glanced at it for a few seconds – and their eyes met.

"Strange," she said.

"Drains," agreed Minna.

"I mean, I can't think how…"

"No, nor can I," said Mum.

"Especially as we don't…"

"No, quite…"

"And never even…"

"No…" said Mum.

"It's so *strange!*" Jeff repeated.

"Drains!" Minna echoed, putting her letter two inches in front of her nose, and peering at it.

Mum looked at Jeff's letter again, and

frowned. "Felicity Harris! Who's Felicity Harris?"

"What do you mean – who is Felicity Harris?"

Mum shrugged. "It says here your name was put forward by a Felicity Harris."

Jeff took the letter in silence, and re-read it. "Felicity Harris…" he murmured. And then the penny dropped. *Dizzi!*

"Uh – hello?" Dizzi's dad (Jeff assumed it was Dizzi's dad) answered the phone. He sounded vague. There was classical music – opera or something – playing loudly in the background.

"Is Dizzi there?" said Jeff.

"*Hello?*" said Mr Harris.

"Is *Dizzi* there?"

"Oh. I'm not… I don't…"

There was the sound of the phone being put down. Jeff waited and waited, listening to the opera-singers. Someone seemed to be upset about something. Someone else seemed to be upset about something else. It didn't, Jeff thought, seem a very relaxing way to spend Saturday morning.

Finally the phone was picked up again. "No. I'm *terribly* sorry. She's gone out."

"Oh."

"Can I take a message?" said Mr Harris.

"Well, tell her Jeff called, and—"

"Oh dear! Wait a second. I have to sharpen my pencil."

Jeff waited until Mr Harris had sharpened his pencil. "Please tell her Jeff called, and—"

"Would that be Jeff with a 'J' or a 'G'?" enquired Mr Harris.

"J," said Jeff. "And—"

"It's just that I have to be very careful with Dizzi's messages," said Mr Harris. "I get into terrible trouble if I get them wrong."

"Oh. OK. Well, ask her to ring me as soon as she gets in, would you?"

An hour later he knew the CaD letter by heart (even the boring bits about parental consent and insurance). But Dizzi still hadn't rung. So he propped the letter against the sugar bowl, pumped up his football, and searched out his old bow and all five arrows. He hadn't done much of his new sport recently. A world champion needed to keep on top of his game...

"Stay in the house, Minna!" he said. "I'm going to be shooting arrows, and I don't want you getting in the way."

"OK, Deff!" said Minna amicably.

Pumping up his football had been a good idea. It was definitely more responsive to a hit. Jeff spent some time refining his points system.

He had just gone back into the kitchen for a biscuit, when he heard Minna's voice. She was in the front hall, and seemed to be talking to someone.

"Inna garden," she said importantly. "Doin' Farchery."

There was a pause.

"Yuss! Farchery!" insisted Minna.

There was another pause.

"Farchery!" yelled Minna.

Jeff dropped the biscuit barrel, and dashed

out to the hall. Minna was standing by the wall-phone, holding the receiver the wrong way up.

"Who are you talking to, Minna?" Jeff said, trying to grab the receiver.

She hugged it tight to her chest, and looked at him crossly. "Try'n to talk!"

"Is it a real person, Minna?" he begged. "Or are you just pretending?"

She gave him a withering look. "Dis a real phone, Deff! Not a 'tend phone! Look!" She opened her hands to show him the receiver.

Jeff grabbed it, and pulled it to his ear. "Hello?" he said.

He just had time to hear Dizzi say, "Jeff?" before the screams started. Jeff put his hand over the receiver, and added his screams to Minna's. *"MUM!"*

"Sorry about that," said Jeff after Mum had scooped Minna up. "She's a pain."

"She's a sweetie. She told me all about you. Said you were in the garden doing something called—"

"I've got some news!" said Jeff.

105

There was a second's pause. "Oh."

"You might well say, 'Oh'."

"*Oh*," said Dizzi again.

"I got a letter, asking me to interview for *Cybernauts*."

"Jeff, that's *amazing*!"

"It is, isn't it?"

"You could be on telly!"

"I could," agreed Jeff. "On a programme I've never even seen."

"I wrote a great letter," said Dizzi happily. "One of my best."

"But why didn't you *tell* me?"

"Because I didn't think you had a chance."

"So why did you do it?"

"Because…a chance is a chance."

Jeff thought a moment. "Dizzi?"

"Yes?"

"Why did you put *me* up for it, and not *you*?"

"Me? Oh, I don't want to do television!" said Dizzi. "I'd hate it."

"Would you?"

"Yes! I'm not a front-of-camera person." She

paused. "I'm an end-of-the-pen person. A fixer."

"What?"

"A fixer. That what my dad calls me. I have ideas and write letters and stuff."

"But...did you tell them I'd never seen *Cybernauts*?"

"No. Of course not! I'm not a complete idiot! Fixers aren't, generally speaking."

"Suppose not."

"But I told them about you coming up to me in the library!" She laughed. "That must have done the trick!"

Jeff wobbled the flex of the telephone. "Oh, Dizzi," he said. "All I ever wanted to do was to see *Cybernauts*. And now I could be *on* it."

There was a short silence. "Aren't you pleased?" said Dizzi.

Jeff thought. "Well, it might be nice for Minna."

"Oh, come on! Wouldn't you like to be on television?" Suddenly there was a slight edge to Dizzi's voice.

"Um..." said Jeff.

Dizzi said nothing.

"Er..." said Jeff.

Dizzi still said nothing.

"Oh, all right...yes!" said Jeff.

Barking

"They just want to make sure you're not completely barking!"

"Maybe I *am* completely barking."

Jeff and Dizzi were sitting in the café opposite the library. They could talk there without having to be quiet.

"You're not completely barking." Dizzi sipped her orange juice. "You're just the sort of person they need."

"Am I?"

"Yes."

"How do you know?"

Dizzi looked at him. "I know!"

Jeff took another slug of his coke.

"So your Mum's OK about driving you there?" asked Dizzi.

Jeff nodded. "It's *watching* television she's

against. Not *being* on television. That seems to be allowed."

Dizzi laughed.

Jeff bit his thumbnail. "What do you think they'll ask me?"

"Oh, you know – school, family, hobbies, that sort of thing." Dizzi frowned. "That reminds me, there's something I keep forgetting to ask. When I rang, Minna said you were doing something called Farchery."

"Ah!" said Jeff. "Did I ever tell you about the time Minna ate a spider?"

Dizzi leant forward. "So what is this Farchery?"

"Oh, nothing!" said Jeff lightly.

Dizzi eyed him. "Come on. Tell me."

"Well, it's a bit difficult to explain."

"That's OK. I'm not going anywhere."

Jeff looked at Dizzi. She hated not knowing things.

"OK," he said. "But you'll laugh."

She did. She pealed with laughter. The two women across the way looked up from their coffees, and smiled.

"I take it all back, Jeff!" said Dizzi between giggles. "You *are* completely barking!"

Dizzi was right. The interview was fine. The worst of it was the long drive to the studios (but at least they didn't have Minna, who had gone to her friend Rufus for the day).

A girl called Bella, in pink cardigan and jeans, fetched him and Mum from reception and took them down a corridor to a little room. Jeff expected Bella to fetch someone else to interview him, but she settled into the chair and started doing it herself.

First it was straightforward questions about age and family, and then Bella wanted to know a bit about schoolwork and hobbies and sport. But that was it.

Jeff had decided that if she asked if he had ever actually seen *Cybernauts*, he would tell the truth. But the strange thing was that she never did...

He got the letter just before Christmas.

"Dizzi?"

"Yes?"

"I've heard."

"And?"

"I'm in."

"You're not."

"I am."

"You're not!"

"*I am*. They want me in January."

"Oh, Jeff you'll be so cu…"

"What?"

"I mean you'll be so cool!"

"Hmmm."

Just before she rang off, Dizzi said, "Oh, and Jeff?"

"Yes."

"You know you're supposed to wear your pyjamas, don't you?"

"*My pyjamas?*"

Dizzi pealed with laughter. "Only kidding!"

Game on

Jeff sat in the studio in pyjamas.

In fact they weren't pyjamas, though they looked a bit like it. Grey with a thin red stripe down each side. On the front and back "JEFF" was printed in big red letters. The five other contestants were in the same type of pyjamas. And each had a silver pack strapped round his or her waist. These were the *Cybernauts* outfits.

All six were sitting in what was called "the prepping area".

They were waiting for some "prepping".

Jeff looked round at the competition. Opposite him sat two boys, "LEE" and a pale boy called "MARTIN", and a red-haired girl called "ANNE-MARIE". Beside him sat two more girls, who were whispering together.

Everyone else seemed a bit older than him, especially Lee, who was huge, but perhaps that was just his imagination. And they all seemed a bit nervous, except Anne-Marie, who was lounging back, sticking out her grey-covered legs and grinning at everyone.

Apart from the whispering girls, no one was saying much. It did seem silly, just sitting there, not talking. So Jeff framed a question in his head ("Are you a big *Cybernauts* fan?"), met Martin's gaze, opened his mouth – and a man with a clipboard appeared. He wore a jacket and tie, and looked very harassed. Was this Baz Haskins? Jeff decided it wasn't. There was nothing at all remarkable about his thinning hair for a start. Dizzi had definitely said there was something about Baz Haskins's hair...

The man with the clipboard introduced himself as Bill, and checked off their names again (which was strange as they *wearing* them). Then he explained what was going to happen, starting with a group line-up on the set. "And, remember," he finished, "try not to

114

look directly at the cameras!"

Martin had now gone from pale-looking to green-looking. Bill glanced at him, and said, "Don't worry, son." He gave a wide smile. "It's gonna be fun! Just enjoy yourself."

This would have been more comforting if Bill had looked less worried himself – or as if he were remotely enjoying himself.

"Any questions?" said Bill finally.

There was silence.

Then Anne-Marie giggled, and asked, "What happens if we need to go to the loo in the middle?"

Bill looked at her. "Oh, that's not a problem – there's a lot more waiting around between levels and stuff than you might think. There are six of you taking part, after all." He grinned. "We haven't yet had a puddle on the floor in *Cybernauts*!" And everyone fell about as if it was the funniest thing they had ever heard.

"Problem on sound, Bill!" someone shouted, racing though the waiting area. Bill gave a groan, then looked back at them. His face was serious. "I think I'm going to let you into a little secret now."

Everyone looked at him.

"*Cybernauts* isn't quite how you see it on TV. It's high budget for a children's – er, young person's programme, but it is not *that* high budget. We have the same basic set every episode – we just have different graphics every time." Bill ran a hand through his thinning hair. "So don't be surprised if parts of the set look...fairly basic. The walls of the corridors are pretty flimsy, for instance. And of course you'll keep seeing scaffolding and cables, and people with lights and microphones. You must do your best to ignore them."

"Bill!" someone shouted. "*Bill!*" And he nodded at them, and was gone.

"Well!" said somebody.

"Christmas!" said Anne-Marie.

"I hope I don't put a foot through one of those flimsy corridors he was talking about," said Lee gloomily, crossing his massive legs. "It'd be just my luck."

"I think I've changed my mind," said the girl

beside Jeff in a little voice – and everyone looked at her before laughing.

Martin caught Jeff's eye. "So are you a big *Cybernauts* fan?"

"No," said Jeff.

"*No?*"

"Anyone like some more hot chocolate?" said Jeff. "I think I saw a machine down there."

There was more hanging around. Then they were fitted with microphones, and tested for sound. Then they went to the green room, and waited a bit more. And – suddenly – it was all happening. They all filed onto the set for a group line-up – and then went and sat at the side, waiting to go on one by one. The girls were called first. Anne-Marie came back, rolling her eyes. Martin was the first boy to be called. And then it was Jeff.

Crunch!

Jeff found himself standing just behind a white strip on the floor, looking at a fuzzy-haired man with a very orange face. Yes, this *had* to be Baz Haskins.

Jeff knew he had to look at Baz, and not the cameras, but it was quite difficult with three of them bearing down on him.

"And this is our sixth contestant, Jeff Wilson. Hi, Jeff!"

"Hi, there!" said Jeff. He was glad to hear his voice sounded pretty normal – not squeaky or anything.

Baz read out some details about Jeff from the autocue, then looked at him, and gave a wink. "Fancy your chances today, Jeff?"

"Er...yes. No. I don't know," stammered Jeff.

Baz snickered. "Don't know, hey? Well, I like a bit of modesty in a chap." He clapped him in a matey way on the shoulder. "Bet you're raring to go, eh? Ready for a bit of cybernetic action?"

Jeff nodded. "I guess."

Baz glanced at the autocue. "And now, *you* didn't put yourself up, did you? You were put up by...let's see, a young lady called Felicity?"

"Yes."

Baz looked at him roguishly. "Is she a *girlfriend?*"

Jeff stared back at him. How dare he ask that? "No, she's just a good friend."

Baz tittered. "That's what they all say, isn't it?"

Jeff said nothing.

Baz laughed, and flung out an arm. "Well, then, you'd better do your best for your good friend Felicity!"

And suddenly Jeff was walking back to his seat. Lee lumbered past him, looking a bit dazed. Jeff shot him a grin.

*

The cameras were running. Three, two, one.

"Listen, my brave Cybernauts!" Baz Haskins was in Commander-mode now. He was wearing a high-collared cloak. "Your mission is to get to a planet, called Kalyx, and take possession of the Omega!" He tapped a silver pointer at a weird map. "Kalyx is situated at the outer corner of the Beta-Z Galaxy."

The Beta-Z Galaxy. Was he supposed to remember this? Jeff frowned, and tried to concentrate.

"If you successfully reach Kalyx, you then have to travel through five different levels. At Level Five, you will find the Omega." The Commander's hair twinkled impressively under the lights. "The Omega has been stolen by the evil Galtenes – which means the whole Universe could be in jeopardy." His eyes swept around the six Cybernauts. "To gain the Omega you will need skill, stamina, courage, intelligence, and quick-thinking..."

It sounded an awfully long list to Jeff.

"Now, remember!" Baz Haskins smirked towards the cameras, then turned back. "You

120

may meet anyone on your travels, and I mean *anyone*. You can trust any Kalicians, old inhabitants of Kalyx. They look like humans. Do not trust Zadians. They are spies for the Galtenes, and look human, but have double ear-lobes. Galtenes – well, the less said about Galtenes, the better. Just pray you don't meet one!"

Someone gave a nervous giggle.

Jeff met Anne-Marie's eye.

Suddenly Haskins flung out an arm. "That is your mission!" His voice wobbled with drama. "Go, and good luck to you all!"

"Yes, Commander," said Anne-Marie (as they had been told, but a bit too early).

"Yes, Commander!" said everyone else.

"Yes, Commander!" said Jeff.

Jeff was staring into space. At asteroid dust.

Asteroid *dust?* This was more like great lumps of the stuff! Jeff swerved to the right to avoid a big craggy bit. The ship moved easily. He was glad he had chosen this nippy light spacecraft, rather than the great freighter.

It was not that difficult. Jeff had played computer games that were far more difficult. In fact it was very similar to playing a game in an arcade, apart from the cameras. All around him, the set was painted blue.

Each Cybernaut was on The Mission alone – and now it was Jeff's turn at the control panel of his chosen spaceship.

He gazed out at the cloud of asteroid pieces projected on the screen.

It seemed to be thinning now.

Good.

He began to relax.

Then something appeared in front of him, slightly to the right. What was it? Certainly not a bit of asteroid. It was…sort of shiny and smooth, metal of some sort, and it was getting bigger and bigger.

Which meant closer and closer…

Jeff snapped into action. He boosted his engines, and tried to swing his ship to the left. It did respond, but reluctantly. He started pulling desperately at the levers, but this made less and less difference. The strange metal object was closer now. Jeff saw that it was some sort of huge craft, or city in the sky. It was clearly exerting a great pull. Was he in some sort of magnetic field? Whatever it was, he was being sucked remorselessly towards the gargantuan object.

Aargh! It looked as if his mission was to be aborted before he had even reached Level One!

Suddenly Jeff had an idea – he'd stop pulling away from the newcomer, which wasn't working anyway. Instead he'd try to turn his craft alongside it, to fly parallel. This seemed to work better...yes! OK, he wasn't getting *away*, but at least he wasn't going to smash against that huge hull. He put his ship to cruise, in the opposite direction to which the alien craft was moving. He couldn't see the end of it at all, he just had to hope there was an end...

There was, too. Suddenly the hull seemed to narrow. Jeff's heart lifted, and then – CRUNCH!

He gasped in shock. What was that?

As the huge metal object slipped away

behind him, the tinny voice of the on-ship computer rang out.

"Damage to ship hull from unidentified object. Damage to ship hull from unidentified object. Cameras moving into place now to bring you pictures of damage."

Jeff waited, biting his lip, until a picture appeared on his screen. There was his ship, and there seemed to be a wide uneven gash, near the stern. Something, from somewhere (a scanner from the huge craft, perhaps) had hit him.

"Is...is the damage much?" he asked the computer.

"Checking..." said the computer. It flashed some lights. "Some damage to hull, but not enough to affect operational efficiency."

Jeff relaxed.

"Crack detected in fuel tank."

"Wha-a-a-at?"

His heart began to pound...

It was strange.

In one way he knew it was only pretend, that he was sitting playing a computer game in a suburban television studio, that he could stop the whole thing at any minute.

But in another way it was real. He was a space envoy. He was on a mission. He was flying through the airless void with a leaking fuel tank. He was in deadly danger.

He drew breath. "Where is the nearest place I can get repairs? And a refuel?"

The computer flashed a light, then answered. "The planet Dorian," it said. "Nine light years away. Do you wish me to set co-ordinates?"

"Yes," said Jeff. Then a thought struck him. "No, not yet. Hang on. This planet Dorian – is it safe?"

"The air is safe to breathe," the computer pinged.

"Good," said Jeff.

"The temperature is within safety levels."

"Good," said Jeff.

"The Dorians kill humans on sight."

"Ah," said Jeff. "Well, I think in that case we had better have a rethink."

*

Arguing with a Giant Lizard

The claw came poking through the grille.

Jeff kept a safe distance from it.

It was a very real claw.

There was probably another on the creature too. Somewhere...

Jeff was getting his fuel tank repaired at a little planet called Ob-Obodan. His on-ship computer had told him the Ob-Obodites were excellent engineers, tolerant of other species, and could even speak basic English. It hadn't told him they were giant lizards.

Jeff looked at a monitor showing a team of lizards flickering over a spaceship, doing repairs. And then he turned back to the grille – and the owner of the very real claws.

"I told you," he said wearily. "I don't have 130 Space Dollars. I only have 100 Space

Dollars." He held the large blue chip towards the scaly snout.

"Den we keep de ship," said the lizard.

Jeff sighed.

He argued with the lizard. He pleaded with the lizard. He told the lizard that he was on a mission that was Vital to the Safety of the Universe, and would pay the extra thirty Space Dollars as soon as he had them. But the lizard was unmoved. The lizard wanted cash up-front.

Jeff was in despair. What was he to do? He hadn't even made it to Level One. He couldn't get anywhere without a vessel.

Suddenly a scaly claw came through the grille again. Jeff leapt back, but the claw was pointing to the silver pack around his waist. "Dat! What else is in dat?" said the lizard.

"Oh!" said Jeff. Why hadn't he thought of something else from the pack? He and the other contestants had spent some time examining them while waiting. He unzipped it again, keeping his 100 Space Dollars tight in his hand, and turned it out on a ledge. There was a small pair of high-tech looking binoculars, a calculator, a gold-coloured necklace, a pencil and pad, a smart silver tool-kit, and a smooth, round stone. The lizard surveyed them with its bright yellow eyes, and then spoke.

"I will take any two of those instead of the thirty Space Dollars."

Great. But *what?* Jeff bit his lip. Suddenly he didn't feel like losing any of his pack items. *Come on, come on!* He must think quickly. But how could he possibly know what he was going to need? And did the lizard know something he didn't?

He picked up the stone, and examined it closely. It really was exactly what it looked like – an ordinary stone. But some instinct told him to hang on to it. It looked so useless, he reasoned, it *had* to be of some use. Then he picked up the gold necklace. There wasn't much you could do with a gold necklace, apart from wear it, was there? No, that could go, even if it was worth more than the other things...

He considered the remaining objects. The pencil and pad, surely? That seemed so…well, *low-tech*, compared with everything else. After all, he was a Cybernaut, wasn't he? And pens and paper – they were old-format tools, weren't they?

He was just about to pick them up, when something Dan had once said jumped into his head. Dan had been talking about the American and Russian space programmes. Both the USA and the Soviets had the same problem – how to write in space, he had explained. So what happened? *The Americans spent billions of dollars developing a ballpoint pen that could write in zero gravity. And the Russians gave their astronaut…a PENCIL!* Jeff could still see Dan's smile of amusement as he said the last word. Such a brilliantly simple answer!

He looked again at the pencil and pad.

All right, it might not exactly be high-tech. But it was still the only means he had of recording information. He picked up the binoculars, and handed them to the waiting claw…

He "travelled" to Kalyx easily after that (he didn't have to go back on the controls). But to get to Level Two, he had to go through a sort of maze. This was mainly painted blue (like the rest of the set), and he had to wear a protective helmet. There was some climbing (a ladder that went up and back), some sliding (a pole), and some crawling (down a narrow winding tunnel). Jeff kept going warily, wondering if something might jump out at him at some stage, but nothing did.

The last challenge was to swing on a rope between two platforms.

They were fairly wide apart, so he walked back to give himself a good run-up, grabbing the rope as high as he could.

He started running. *Now!* He held the rope tight with both hands – and leapt. There was a sudden jerk on his arms as they took his weight – and then he was swinging, surprisingly slowly, towards the other platform. He couldn't see below him (his arm seemed to be in the way). So he just let go at the widest swing of the arc. He tensed his legs for the platform, and felt it – smack! – below his feet. *Touchdown!*

This was the end of the maze. After a break to get his breath, Jeff was off again (minus the helmet). He had to walk along a long blue walkway. His arms were still a bit sore from swinging on the rope. He walked slowly, carefully. What was in store next? Two-lobed Zadian spies? A cohort of pray-you-don't-meet-them Galatenes? Bob Haskins's hair?

He turned a corner, and saw in front of him...a hotel reception desk. A perfectly ordinary hotel reception desk. And behind the perfectly ordinary reception desk was a perfectly ordinary receptionist. She was blonde, heavily made-up, and wore a neat, brown suit. Beside her on the desk stood a big square panel of keys.

Jeff walked slowly up to the desk. The receptionist's ear-lobes looked perfectly normal.

The receptionist smiled. "Can I help you, Sir?"

He looked at her. There was a label on the

front of her jacket that said, "Alma".

"I want to get to Level Three," he said.

"Yes, Sir!" Alma waved her hand towards the panel of keys beside her. "Help yourself."

Jeff looked from her to it. "You mean, take my own key?"

"Not key! *Keys!*" said Alma.

"Keys?" Jeff looked more closely at the panel. It was lit up, and he could see key heads embedded in even rows. "But how do I know which are the right ones?"

"You don't, Sir!" said Alma. "You just take as many as possible."

"As many as possible? Well, I'll take them all, then."

Alma shook her head. "You can't. You can only take one from each row."

"One from each row." Jeff considered the panel, frowning. Something was niggling at the back of his mind. Then he turned to Alma. "Well, perhaps you could help me? I really need to get through to Level Three."

"Sorry, Sir! Helping is not allowed!" Alma gave a little smile.

What did that little smile mean? Jeff thought back to the giant lizard. He was sorry he had given away the gold necklace now. If he was going to bribe Alma, that was the most likely thing to persuade her. He could see she wasn't wearing a necklace. Rats!

Jeff looked at the panel, and its eight-by-eight rows of keys.

Then he looked at her.

Then he looked at the panel again.

And then he began to smile. "I know this! It's a chess puzzle!"

"Whatever you say, Sir."

He scrabbled in his pack for his pen and pencil. "I can get eight keys max! But I just need to work it out!"

Alma bowed her head.

Jeff grabbed his pen and pad, and feverishly made an eight-by-eight graph. Then he started filling in squares. It was just like the eight queens' puzzle Mum had set him, but he had forgotten the solution. Here? Or that square there? Heart beating, he looked towards Alma. She stood at the desk, perfectly calm.

Suddenly Jeff wondered why he was rushing. He had tried to hurry at the spaceship repair station, but had that been necessary? Nobody had ever mentioned a time limit. He drew a breath, and went on filling in the squares he needed. (OK, the sight of him puzzling over his pad wouldn't be great television, but that wasn't his problem. They would probably edit it – or have exciting music. It would have to be *very* exciting music!)

Finally, when he was sure he'd got it right, he stepped up and pulled at one of his chosen keys. It came out of the panel quite easily, and, as it did so, the light of the other keys in those rows went out. He pulled at one of the keys on the same line experimentally, but it was now stuck fast.

He looked at his solution and went on carefully pulling out keys, till he had eight in his hand. He put them carefully into his silver pack.

When he looked up, Alma had disappeared.

Level Four

"*And tension is mounting! Let's see how Jeff, our youngest contestant, is getting on. Ah, he's got to the portal into Level Three. And he's looking fairly confident too. What a player! But will he have enough keys to open the portal?*

"*There! He's got some keys from his pack, and is fitting them into the locks. One, two, three, four, he's doing well, but will he have enough? Five, six, seven and…yes, EIGHT!*"

The eight keys got Jeff through the portal. First it was a bit stiff to open, and then it was a bit wobbly. But open it did…

Now for the Third Level. He zipped his pack up carefully, and looked around. There was a blue walkway to his right. He straightened his shoulders, and started walking into the blueness…

He was expecting something nasty.

He really was, now.

But he didn't know what.

He walked cautiously towards a corner, which had lights playing on it, making strange shapes on the walls. He reached the corner, turned left – and blinked. In front of him the walkway opened into a wider area, across which streamed bright white lights.

He crept closer.

There seemed to be laser-beams crossing the width of the room, then snapping off, while others appeared somewhere else. He quickly realised what he had to do – run between the lasers to the safety of the other side.

He drew a deep breath.

And then someone appeared.

He was a young man dressed in green, with thick black hair to his shoulders.

"Hi there!" he said with a friendly grin. "I'm Gelph, a guide to this part of the planet."

Jeff eyed him cautiously. "Hello…Gelph."

Gelph nodded towards the lasers. "You won't get through the Running Beams without my help. I've seen a lot try, and they all failed."

Was he talking about the other Cybernauts?

Gelph put his head on one side, and eyed Jeff. "I'll take you – if you can pay me."

"Pay you? How?" said Jeff.

"A metamorph." There was something strangely familiar about Gelph's voice.

"What?"

Gelph looked at him. "I only accept payment in metamorphs."

"I don't have any," said Jeff.

"Are you sure?" said Gelph.

Jeff thought of the things in his pack. Metamorph... Could his pebble be a metamorph...? Slowly he drew it out.

Gelph's eyes lit up. "That's one!"

Jeff's heart leapt. He was glad he had kept the useless-looking stone now.

He was just about to hand it over – when an instinct stayed him. Something wasn't quite right. Gelph had so quickly turned the conversation from whether he should guide him to how he should be paid. Maybe he was a Zadian spy, one of the people Baz Haskins had warned against. Did all that black hair hide a double ear-lobe?

"No!" said Jeff suddenly. "I've changed my mind – I'll try on my own."

"You're a fool then!" Gelph's eyes glittered. "No one can get past the Running Beams without my help. No one!" And he was gone.

Jeff looked towards the Running Beams. Maybe he had blown it. They did look pretty scary. What would they do if he went into them? Cut him in half? That wouldn't be much fun, even if it wasn't for real…

He scratched his head. Maybe he had made a mistake. Maybe he did need Gelph. But there was nothing for it now. He was on his own…

For some time Jeff just stood at the edge, studying the lights. After a bit he could see a sort of pattern emerging. The sequence of laser lights was repeated at regular intervals.

There was a long sequence that was quite clearly an impossible barrier. But directly after this was a period of about seven or eight seconds, when there would be a clear path if he jogged at a slowish rate to start with, then speeded up just after halfway through. He studied the sequence several more times. He would have to set his speed very accurately, he could see that. But it *was* possible, wasn't it?

Well, Jeff, thought, there was only one way to find out. He waited for his moment, drew a deep breath and started jogging.

Take it easy now...set a good pace. Steady, you're through the first few beams. Now keep the pace for a few more steps. That's it... Now begin to speed up. Aaaargh! Stop! A laser's just shot centimetres in front. Don't even wobble! Now it's gone, so off, at a smarter pace this time. Yes...yes...yes...yes!

Suddenly, he was out the other side, heart thumping...

Phew! He must be on Level Four now. Only one to go...

Maths! Jeff stood and stared. That was how he was going to get to Level Five. The portal to Level Five was a maths problem! He certainly hadn't expected this. Ryan and Ben and Al had described *Cybernauts* more as a "Shoot-'Em-Up" than anything else. There had certainly been no mention of maths...

The portal was actually quite impressive.

It was covered with a pattern like a computer circuit board. Lights flashed on and off around the edge.

Right at the centre of the circuit board was a sum.

Jeff goggled. It was so easy!

"111+1001=" And then there was a row of five blanks. Why, he could do it in his head! It was...1112.

He looked to see how he could put the answer in. There were two buttons like on a calculator, saying "0" and "1". But that was all. No "2", or anything higher.

Jeff frowned. Perhaps it just meant he had to do it to the nearest figure? That would be...1111. That had to be it. Suddenly he felt tired. He wanted to get on with it, finish the mission – it seemed to have gone on a long time now. He raised his hand to press the "1" button – and froze. He thought back to that day in the library, the day he had grumpily looked at a book on computers. Of course. That maths language with only "0"s and "1"s. He had forgotten its name – but that was what was being used now, surely! He got out his notepad again, and worked out the sum slowly. Then, just to make sure, he converted it to "ordinary" (7+9), and back again.

When he was quite sure he had got it right, he punched the answer into the buttons. "10,000". As he got to the last "0", the portal slipped noiselessly open...

As he did so Bill stepped over a cable with his clipboard.

"Right!" he said. "We'll set you up for the battle."

Going into Battle

"Yes, yes, oh yes! He's nearly there! Jeff, our careful young operator with the cheeky grin, has got through to the Fifth Level! He had bad luck in the beginning when his spacecraft crashed, but he didn't let that put him off. And he's solved problems that have stumped some of our older contestants. Now he has to battle with the Galtene Warriors..."

Jeff realised that this must be the big one – the set piece.

He was given a break, and a drink, new batteries for his mike transmitter – and a quick briefing.

Bill explained that he was never going to see any Galtene Warriors. That was going to come from the computer graphics. All he would see was green lights, which would turn red when he "killed" one. And he had to kill all the warriors of the cohort in 300 seconds. After this time, the rest of the Galtenes would be alerted, and he would be hopelessly outnumbered.

He was handed a "laser-sword", which had a small red light on its handle, and then there he was, facing…a big screen. It was white and curved, rather like the top half of a satellite dish. Away to one side was a lit-up dial, reading "300".

Three…two…one.

The dial clicked to "299".

He had better get on.

Holding his laser-sword out in front of him, Jeff advanced warily.

Nothing happened for a bit, and then a green light came humming from the right hand side of the screen, getting bigger and bigger.

Jeff stepped forward smartly, pointed his sword at it, and pressed the laser-button – bzzzz! The light rapidly turned to red, then faded away…

Phew! Well, he'd got one!

Then he heard a hum, and saw, out of the corner of his eye, another green light coming in high and right at the edge of the screen. So he leapt sideways, swept his weapon back, and buzzed the laser. Bingo!

The seconds dial showed "256".

They were now starting to come from all sides. He had to move quickly around the screen, but apart from that, it really wasn't difficult. In fact, if it wasn't for the seconds dial, now at "233" he would be quite enjoying himself. At one moment he even disposed of two green lights together. Buzz, buzz!

Really, he thought. Galtene Warriors seemed to be easier to fight than Minna, who went in for biting and hair-pulling...

Suddenly a green light moved quickly over a section of screen and disappeared before he could hit it.

Blast! The red light went out on his laser-sword, and when he pressed the laser buzzer, it wasn't working! Suddenly the screen was swarming with green lights, and the humming was getting louder and louder. And he was defenceless!

One hundred and eighty-six on the dial. Well, he wasn't just going to stand there. There was a pretend rock behind him and to the side. Jeff had assumed it was just part of the set. But it was better than nothing! He ran back as quickly as he could, and knelt behind it, heart beating hard. Nothing happened. Really, he thought, the Galtene Warriors weren't very bright, were they? He licked his lips. They were feeling very dry now, after so much time on the set…

After a few seconds there, his laser-button started working again, so he advanced again on the screen. Sixty-nine said the dial.

Soon he was back at work, demolishing green lights. Buzz…buzz…buzz! Red, red, red!

Then suddenly all the green lights stopped coming. And Jeff stopped too, and just stood, facing the screen. The seconds dial said "8". Had he done it? Was it all over? Would someone tell him what to do now? And then some sixth sense told him to turn round.

He got a shock.

There, three metres or so away, about level with his eyes, was a bright green light. He blinked. How had it got there? But Jeff had no time for wondering this. The bright green light was growing...

He whipped up his laser-sword, and pressed the laser-button as hard as he could. Nothing happened for a second or two. And then the green light swayed slightly. Heartened, he zapped it again. And the green light turned to red. And then went off altogether.

Suddenly a whole series of lights flashed on and off and on again. And then stopped. The battle was finished. Jeff turned to look at the seconds dial. It read "3". He had just made it...

He tucked his laser-sword into his silver belt. He was getting his breath back now. He looked around, and over to his left there seemed to be some sort of cloud forming. He walked cautiously towards it, aware of cameras moving in. He realised now that it wasn't a cloud, it was dry ice. And as he moved through the white swirls, closer to the source, he saw some sort of dais. He walked towards it and climbed the few steps up as if he was in a dream. On a high table, on a stand, stood a strange metallic shape. The Omega.

He licked his lips, and stepped forward.

His heart was thumping now.

He was aware of a camera zooming in on him.

Then he stretched out, and picked up the Omega.

"So how does it feel to be a Saviour of the Universe?" asked Mum.

"Oh, pretty good," said Jeff.

They were in the car on the way back.

It was late.

It had taken some time to get away from the studios. Anne-Marie had insisted on kissing Jeff, and then the other girls had to kiss him too. Martin had gone on and on about why it was so unfair he only got to Level One. ("Take no notice – he wussed out!" Anne-Marie had whispered.) Lee had fallen at the swing rope, but seemed quite cheerful.

"I saw quite a bit, actually." Mum was slowing at some traffic lights. "But I gather it will make much more sense once they add the graphics." She laughed. "Apparently there's even a cyber-audience!"

"Mmm," said Jeff. "I'd like to see those Galtene Warriors I defeated."

"Did you defeat some Galtene Warriors?" said Mum.

"Yes, I *did!*" said Jeff. "Do concentrate, Mum!"

"Oh. Sorry."

"I hope the graphics people make them look really scary."

"They will. They transform it, apparently. I just don't know how they get everything in."

"Oh, they edit like mad for the best bits," said Jeff.

"I see. I think." Mum moved off as the traffic lights turned to green.

Jeff fingered his Cybernauts Trophy. It was surprisingly light for its size, but looked very impressive. He could just see it on his bookcase. Or maybe in the front room, instead of the *Fatsia Japonica*. Where the television used to be…

"What are you going to say to Dizzi?" asked Mum. "Are you going to tell her you won?"

"We're not supposed to tell anyone." Jeff stared out at the yellow street lights.

Dizzi would want to know what had happened.

Dizzi would *definitely* want to know what had happened.

And Dizzi always seemed to get her own way.

Maybe she ought to get her way on this. Or maybe for once she ought *not*.

He made his decision. "No, I won't tell her."

"Good for you." Mum's voice changed. "Now, I must concentrate – make sure we don't miss our turning."

Jeff began to doze off. Soon they were onto a faster road.

"At least the traffic's OK now," said Mum. "We should be back in an hour. A good thing

Minna's staying the night at Granny's." A tinge of worry crept into her voice. "I hope everything's OK."

"Are you worried about Minna?" said Jeff.

"Well...I think I'm more worried about Granny!"

Jeff laughed, and snoozed off again.

Suddenly Mum spoke again. "Do you know when it's going to be on?"

"What?"

"*Cybernauts*, of course!"

"Surprisingly quickly, I think," he said sleepily. "Something fell off the schedules or something."

There was silence.

"You know what?" said Mum.

"What?"

"We'll have to get a television now, won't we?"

He raised his head from the seat-back. "We *will*?"

"Yes."

Yay! Though why wasn't he feeling even more elated? "You don't mind, do you?" *Why was he asking that?*

"Not, really." Mum glanced over at him. "I always meant to get the telly back some time. Actually I've sort of missed it."

"You *have?*"

"Yes. It was fun seeing those films at Granny's at Christmas, wasn't it?"

"Sure was!"

"There *are* good things on telly. As a matter of fact something good is coming up quite soon."

Her words hung in the air for a bit.

"Er...? Oh! Yeah!"

Mum laughed. "I have to give it to you, Jeff. You've forced my hand quite brilliantly!"

"Yup." Jeff burrowed back into his seat. He had done a good day's work that day. He had Saved the Universe – and got the television back as well...

Fairy Cake

Had it all really happened?

Jeff dressed slowly the next morning.

Perhaps it – *Cybernauts* – hadn't happened at all. After all nothing seemed to be changed.

Jeff slipped on his school shoes, once so new and now so scuffed-looking.

He had his usual breakfast (a slice of toast), left at his usual time (8.05am), and made his usual way to school through the grey January day. School went on just as usual too. (No one even asked why he had missed school the day before.) The only thing that was even slightly out of the ordinary was a charity cake sale, organised by Alison Pringle.

"Cakes, cakes, cakes – I want cakes!" Ryan was chanting as they waited for Mr Dawson.

During the lesson, Jeff watched the clock

tick slowly up to the hour hand. And when the bell went, he leapt up to join the stampede. But Mr Dawson beckoned him over.

"I don't seem to have your last history assignment, Jeff."

Homework. Jeff looked at Dawson. Did Saviours of the Universe do history homework? Dawson looked back at him. Yes, Jeff thought, perhaps Saviours of the Universe *did* do history homework. "Sorry – you'll definitely have it tomorrow!"

Mr Dawson nodded his head. "I look forward to seeing it."

Jeff bolted.

But it was too late. Everything in the cake sale – every last flapjack – had been sold. The tables were bare. Jeff turned away in disgust, and made his way to his friends, who were standing by the swing door. Ben was crumpling a wrapper and Al was wiping his mouth with his sleeve. Ryan was wolfing the remains of something chocolatey.

"Hey!" said Jeff.

They looked up at him.

"Did you get something for me?"

Ryan put the last of whatever it was into his mouth.

"Sorry!" said Ben, spraying out chocolate crumbs.

"We barely got stuff for us!" said Al.

"It was a bun fight!" said Ryan.

"Some people are so greedy!" said Ben.

"The chocolate brownies were good," said Ryan.

"Alison Pringle made them," said Ben.

"She never uses a mix," said Ryan.

"It's a good cause, too," Al said piously.

Jeff slumped back against the door.

Some friends!

Then he looked up – and saw Henry. Henry was standing the other side of the swing doors. He was waving something at him. "You can have this if you like."

"What is it?" he said.

"A fairy cake."

"A *fairy* cake?"

"Yup." Henry grinned. "But if that's a problem, you could call it a bun."

"No problem, mate," said Jeff. "Fairy cake it is." And he took it, tore off the paper and bit into it gratefully. As he munched, he eyed Henry.

All right, Henry was not the coolest guy in the class. But he gave you fairy cakes. Anyway, did he *want* to be friends with the coolest guy in the class?

Suddenly he felt a punch on his arm. He turned.

"Great news, Jeff!" Ryan was grinning.

"Yes?" said Jeff. "What?"

Ben started humming the *Cybernauts* tune.

"There's going to be..." Ryan spread his hands. "A new series of..."

"*Cybernauts*!" said Al.

"Good, yah?" said Ben in a silly accent.

Ryan looked at Henry. "Did you see the first series?"

Henry shrugged. "I caught it once or twice."

Ryan slung an arm around Jeff's shoulders. "More than this guy did." He sniggered. "Ain't got a television."

Henry's expression didn't change.

"I know."

Ryan stared at him. "Well, you gotta have television! I mean, you can't *survive* without television!"

Henry looked at Jeff. "He seems alive," he said. "Yup. Definitely alive."

Ryan's eyes suddenly seemed to glaze. "Er...well, I guess we'd better be off. Got to find some *people*."

Henry gazed after the departing trio with a lop-sided smile. Then he turned to Jeff. "People, eh? I wonder what he thought we were!" he said.

And Jeff fell about laughing. It was definitely the best laugh he had had in school for a long time. "Come on," he said to Henry. "Let's get outside. We've still some time before the bell goes."

They went out together. And found themselves talking about baseball and basketball, and the new art teacher and the best glue for wood, and Alison Pringle's hair...

OK, Jeff thought, as walked inside with

Henry. Henry was never going to be a Dan. There was only one Dan after all. Dan was a one-off. But there was still quite a lot going for Henry...

The Watchers

Ryan opened the door "Come on in. Ben's already here."

"Cool!"

"Grab a can, Al. It's just about to start."

"Cheers, Ryan!"

"Ssh! It's just starting."

"Hope they haven't changed it."

"Hope they've made it a bit different."

"Might be some surprises."

"Bound to be some surprises..."

Ben balanced on a space-hopper, and the other two settled down on the sofa.

The opening credits came to a close.

Baz Haskins bounced onto the screen, big-haired and grinning.

"Welcome to a new series of Cybernauts. And have we got some cyber-entertainment for you tonight!" The camera zoomed in on his face. "First of all – let's meet our six young contestants."

Ryan stirred. "Wish we'd fixed to go on to this."

Al nodded. "Should have written in."

"Didn't you say you'd find the address, Al?" said Ben.

"Uh-uh. I think that was you."

Ben wobbled on his space-hopper.

The camera panned over six grey-suited figures.

"Hey! He looked a bit like Jeff Thingie!" said Ryan, laughing.

"Perhaps it was Jeff," said Al.

"Nah," said Ryan.

"Dead ringer, though, wasn't he?"

"Not really. This one was taller," said Ryan.

"And older," said Ben.

"And cooler," said Ryan.

"Poor old Jeff, what a loser!" said Ben.

The camera was now back on Baz Haskins. He started introducing each Cybernaut in turn. The first was a red-headed girl called

Anne-Marie, who looked very nervous. Then came two more girls. Then a heavily-built boy called Lee, who gazed rather gloomily at the camera.

"What a lard-butt!" said Ryan, cramming crisps into his mouth, and following up with a sloosh of coke.

Then Baz read out the next Cybernaut's name. "Next we have our youngest contestant…Jeff Wilson!"

Al's mouth fell open.

Ryan splurted coke and crisps everywhere.

And Ben fell off his space-hopper.

They all goggled at the screen, as Jeff walked up to Baz.

"Hi, Jeff!" said Baz, on the screen.

"Hi there!" said Jeff, on the screen.

And the room erupted.

Henry wasn't really looking at the television. He was really learning his French verbs. His sister Emma, sitting by his feet against the sofa, was watching something. It was about sick animals. There seemed to be a white fluffy *thing and a green scaly thing. As far as Henry could tell, the white fluffy thing was getting much more air-time than the green scaly thing...*

His mum came and sat next to him with her mug of tea, saying, "Budge up, Hen."

He shuffled along the sofa, and placed his hand down one column of the verbs. "Um...mettre, mis...capitre, capis..."

A few minutes later, a theme tune blared out, and he glanced vaguely towards the screen. Oh, yes, that cyber computer-graphic thing was on. Someone had been going on about it at school recently, hadn't they?

He looked up again to see that big-haired presenter who always did the programme...what was it called? Yes, Cybernauts. *Henry frowned. Who was it who had been going on about* Cybernauts...?

Ryan Fuller? No, there was Jeff, suddenly in close-up, on the screen, so perhaps it was Jeff...

He glanced back at his French irregular verbs, and...Jeff on the screen? JEFF? ON THE

*SCREEN? DRESSED IN A CYBER-SUIT WITH HIS
NAME IN BIG LETTERS!*

*It couldn't be. But it was. IT WAS. Henry
gazed in disbelief. It was extraordinary to see
Jeff's familiar face looking out over his own
front room.*

*He waved his French book at the television.
"That boy there. He's called Jeff."*

*"Well done, Henry," said Emma. "It's
wonderful being able to read, isn't it?"*

*"No, I know him! He's called Jeff Wilson. He's
a friend of mine at school."*

"Really?" His mum laughed. "Truly?"

"Yup!"

"Mmm!" said Emma. "He looks quite cute!"

"Ssh!" said Henry. "I want to listen!"

*"I didn't know you had a friend called Jeff!"
said Mum.*

"You don't know all my friends."

"Can I have his autograph?" said Emma.

"No! Shush!"

*His mum nudged him in the ribs. "Don't tell
me he's a friend all of a sudden, just because
he's on telly."*

Henry stared at the screen, and considered. "No," he said. "He was a friend already. Even before tonight."

Dizzi looked up from the screen with stars in her eyes. "Jeff won, Jeff won!"

"So it would seem," said Mr Harris, polishing his glasses.

"He won, he WON!"

"Deservedly, too, in my opinion. Though it was, you must admit, rather an absurd contest."

"HE WON! HE WON!" Dizzi bounced up and down on the sofa. "I guessed he'd done well, but he wouldn't tell me. Wouldn't! Though I badgered and badgered and badgered!"

"The more I see and hear of your friend Jeff," said Mr Harris, "the more I approve."

They both turned back to the screen, as the credits rolled, and a spaceship zoomed off into purple skies.

"And I did it," Dizzi half-whispered to herself.

"Yes, Dizzi," said her father. "It seems you did." He put his glasses back on, and looked at her. *"As I have said before, and no doubt will again, you are a fixer."*

Dizzi hugged herself. "I am, aren't I?"

"I'll be interested to see what you pull off next."

"Yes," said Dizzi. "So will I!"

Jeff and Mum and Minna watched on the brand new television set (the *Fatsia Japonica* shimmered away in its new position by the window).

All three were silent as the credits began to roll.

Then Mum said, "Wow! It was something with those graphics, wasn't it?"

Jeff nodded. "Yup! Sure was!"

"I loved the big fight at the end. My little Jeff, defeating those huge horrible things!"

Jeff laughed. "As if!"

Mum put an arm around him "You know something?"

"What?"

"I'm proud of you, Jeff," said Mum. "I really am."

Jeff couldn't help a smile curling across his face. He shrugged. "Hey! At least I got to watch an episode!"

Mum laughed. "Yup!" She picked up the remote control, and turned off the telly.

Jeff looked at her. "It's not going in your cupboard now, is it?"

"No!" said Mum. "But…we get to be choosy!"

"Choosy?"

"Yup! Only watch the good stuff! OK?"

Jeff thought, and nodded. "OK! Choosy is good!"

Choosy was good.

And not just about television programmes.

About friends, too.

He thought about Henry. He wished now he'd told him about the programme.

And he thought about Dizzi…

Minna had been very silent. Now she looked up at Mum. "Dat was Deff on de telly," she half-stated, half-asked.

"Yes, Minna," said Mum, "it was."

Minna turned to Jeff. "Dat was you on de telly, Deff!"

He smiled at her. "Yes, Minna," he said. "I know."

Minna looked at Mum. "D'you like da telly now Deff is onnit?"

Mum smiled. "Yes, Minna."

"And you, Deff?"

He looked down at her and smiled. "It's OK," he said. "Sometimes. But there's lots of other good stuff to do."

The phone went.

"Bet that's Dizzi!" said Mum.

And it was.

More Red Apples to get your teeth into...

What Howls at the Moon in Frilly Knickers?

e. f. smith

1 84121 808 1   £4.99

"Let's write a joke book!"

It was just one of those ideas that took off. Julian and
his friends thought writing a joke book would be easy.
But hundreds of corny **groan-out-loud**
jokes later, they're not so sure...

This hilarious and touching story, full of everyone's
favourite old jokes – and some new ones! – is
guaranteed to have you **howling with laughter**.

"Sensitive and lighthearted. Kids will love it. And if you
must know, it's an underwear-wolf!" **Books for Keeps**

"This book gloriously manages to be both sad and funny."
Booktrust 100 Best Books

1 84121 539 2   £4.99

Jason's Aunt Hester is a grouchy old stick.
But a witch? Surely not?
But then, why is there a whole crew of pirates
held prisoner in her cellar...?

Aided by Scuttle, the saltiest, smelliest seadog ever,
Jason sets out to solve the mystery and defeat
the evil Skegglewitch.

Something's after Jiggy McCue!
Something big and angry and invisible.
Something which hisses and flaps and stabs
his bum and generally tries to make
his life a misery. Where did it come from?

Jiggy calls together the Three Musketeers
– One for all and all for lunch! –
and they set out to send the poltergoose
back where it belongs.

Shortlisted for the Blue Peter Book Award

1 84121 713 1 £4.99

The underpants from hell – that's what Jiggy calls them, and not just because they look so gross. No, these pants are evil. And they're in control. Of him. Of his life! Can Jiggy get to the bottom of his problem before it's too late?

"...the funniest book I've ever read."

Teen Titles

"Hilarious!"

The Independent

Winner of the Stockton Children's Book of the Year Award

1 84121 752 2   £4.99

**Feel like your life has gone down the pan?
Well here's your chance to swap it
for a better one!**

**When those tempting words appear on the
computer screen, Jiggy McCue just can't
resist. He hits "F for Flush" and...Oh dear.
He really shouldn't have done that. Because
the life he gets in place of his own is a very
embarrassing one – for a boy.**

"Fast, furious and full of good humour."
National Literacy Association
"Altogether good fun." *School Librarian*
"Hilarity and confusion." *Teen Titles*

Michael Lawrence

1 84121 756 5   £4.99

Jiggy McCue wants some good luck
for a change.
But instead of luck he gets a genie.
A teenage genie who turns against him.
Then the maggoty dreams start.
Dreams which, with his luck and this genie,
might just come true.

"Will have you squirming with horror and delight!"
Ottakars 8-12 Book of the Month
"Funny, wacky and lively."
Cool-reads

Orchard Red Apples

All books priced at £4.99

Orchard Red Apples are available from all good bookshops,
or can be ordered direct from the publisher:
Orchard Books, PO BOX 29, Douglas IM99 1BQ
Credit card orders please telephone 01624 836000 or fax 01624 837033
or visit our Internet site: www.wattspub.co.uk
or e-mail: bookshop@enterprise.net for details.

To order please quote title, author and ISBN
and your full name and address.
Cheques and postal orders should be made payable to 'Bookpost plc.'
Postage and packing is FREE within the UK
(overseas customers should add £1.00 per book).

Prices and availability are subject to change.